Nine Days

Also by Toni Jordan

Addition
Fall Girl

Nine Days

Toni Jordan

SCEPTRE

First published in Australia by The Text Publishing Company 2012
First published in Great Britain in 2013 by Sceptre
An imprint of Hodder & Stoughton
An Hachette UK company

1

A CIP catalogue record for this title is available from the British Library

Hardback ISBN 978 1 444 76355 3
eBook ISBN 978 1 444 76356 0

Printed and bound by Clays Ltd, St Ives plc

Hodder & Stoughton policy is to use papers that are natural, renewable and
recyclable products and made from wood grown in sustainable forests. The logging
and manufacturing processes are expected to conform to the environmental
regulations of the country of origin.

Hodder & Stoughton Ltd
338 Euston Road
London NW1 3BH

www.sceptrebooks.co.uk

For Robbie,
for everything, of course.

Author note

This novel was inspired by a photograph from the State Library of Victoria's *Argus* newspaper collection of war photographs. The couple in the photograph are unidentified. Connie Westaway and Jack Husting are entirely fictitious and their fates are not those of the photograph's subjects.

CHAPTER ONE

Kip

 SOME DAYS ONE hint of light peeking through the curtains and bam! You spring out of bed like the devil's after you, like you've been lying there all night just waiting for the day to begin so your legs can move. They're itchy and nervy, busting to get going, like you're sitting in the pictures waiting for the film to start. *What's going to happen today?* you think. That's how it mostly is. So I should of known by the way I didn't want to get up that things were bound to go wrong. The blankets were pressing on top of me, like they were saying *Kip! Don't move if you know what's good for you!*

I look over at Ma in the other bed: she's dead asleep facing the wall, a mound under her blanket and a pile of coats and

1

jumpers and even Dad's old clothes pulled out of drawers. Francis is squished next to me, his mouth open all pink and white, teeth like headstones planted in marshmallow. He sounds like a cow that swallowed a whistle. His pillow's dripping drool. It's bad luck for me and Ma, sharing a room with Francis. Connie's lucky. She has the camp bed in the laundry on account of young ladies needing more privacy than boys or mothers. Get a load of that snoring! One day some poor girl'll have to marry him and she'll never have another decent night's sleep as long as she lives. The bags under her eyes'll be big enough to pack for a weekend at Dromana. Just look at him. The great white hope. It's all right for Francis because he doesn't need to get up for a good two hours and I'm supposed to be real quiet in case I disturb his royal genius-ness but he could do with some disturbing if you ask me.

It's not going to get any easier and it's like diving in the Yarra it's that cold so I pretend I'm Mawson and get dressed quick as, and then tiptoe past Mrs Keith's room because she sleeps to nearly ten then I'm out the back door where my boots are waiting. The air slaps me in the face, wakes me up good and proper. Soon it'll be pinky-light, twinkly-light and the stars will turn in for a bit of a nap themselves but now in the cold dark you can feel the great city waking. If I looked down the side, past the gate to Rowena Parade, I'd see men in their dirty boots and worn coats wrapped tight, heading round the corner, down Lennox Street and across Swan to the IXL factory, or a bit further along to Bryant and May. I can almost hear the tramp of them, boots on bluestones, caps pulled over ears. Those blokes are the workers. There's a whole different lot in white shirts and ties and waistcoats and hats with newspapers under their arms who also walk down Lennox to Swan to catch a tram to the city. Our house here in Rowena Parade is the spot where blokes get divided into proper workers and office men.

Me, I'm one of the proper workers. You can smell every factory in Richmond from our little backyard when the wind's right. Between the end of the footy finals and Easter the hot sweet of the jam hits you first, then the tomato sauce, next burning malt and hops. Now in the middle of winter there's nothing but the tannery and the Yarra, and it's like the dunny cart had a permanent spot in the lane so I'm not standing around to breathe it in.

In our yard, grass finds its way through the bricks laid flat and the cracks in the path. The grass is white-tipped and it crackles under my feet. I'm King Kong, squashing native huts. Crunch crunch. Sorry natives. Then I'm out the gate and into the lane and around the corner and I undo the latch at the Hustings'.

Inside I swing open the top half of the stable door and there he is, Charlie the fire-breathing dragon. He nods, then shakes his head like he's got water in his ears. This is Horse for glad to see me. I rub my palms together and breathe on them because as Ma says *Kip it's not funny to put cold hands on someone's warm body* by which she means *especially not on Francis's backside under his nightshirt first thing in the morning.* We have different ideas of funny, Ma and me. Anyhow, Francis started it.

When my hands are warm I pat the crooked star between

3

Charlie's eyes and then I scratch behind his ears and he pushes his head into my hand and stamps his feathered feet. Keep going, he's saying. More pats, more scratches. Charlie is the smartest horse in the entire universe so he starts snuffling down my sleeve. He always picks the right pocket. Charlie is never wrong. Today: one shrivelled apple from the lane, minus one small bite. Union dues, I tell him. A little deducted for the good of the working man, namely me. I hold the apple flat on my hand and it tickles, then up it goes into his gob and two bites later it's gone.

'Well old boy,' I say. 'We can't stand around here all day when there's work to be done.'

He nods and whinnies to show he's heard me. Before Mr Husting comes out I get the bucket and top up the trough from the pump on the other side of the yard, measure out the oats and close the hay bin tight because one little mouse gets in once and they never let you hear the end of it. While Charlie's eating I sweep out the stable and take the manure to the pile. Charlie's got good bowels as my nan would say. My nan talks a lot about respect especially my lack of same but there's only two types of people she's keen on. The King and Queen Elizabeth and the princesses whose pictures she cuts out of the *Women's Weekly* and sticks up on the kitchen wall, and people with good bowels. I imagine they use the King's bowel habits to time the changing of the guard.

I brush Charlie down till he's shiny. Long straight strokes. He likes this. Mr Husting always says first impressions count, my lad! I'd sooner go out in my nightshirt than have the customers see Charlie not looking his Sunday best. I step into the yard and right on time Mr Husting's coming out the back door in his suit and knitted vest and his gloves with no fingers. He looks tired. His cheeks are longer. He says good morning and asks after Charlie.

'He's beaut, Boss.'

'Good lad, Kip.' He reaches out his hand and messes my hair, which is something I allow very few people the latitude to do on account of I'm fourteen now, not a kid anymore, but being boss gives Mr Husting certain privileges.

'That horse looks fighting fit. Better than Catalogue.' And then Mr Husting holds his other hand out flat and instead of an apple there's a shilling. 'For you, Kip.'

Whacko! A whole entire shilling is enough to get in to the Glaciarium, if I shrink down a bit. Skating on ice. Just imagine it. Maybe today will turn out all right after all. The trick will be to put my shilling where Francis won't find it. I need a hiding place like Connie's, a loose brick under the house. She doesn't know I'm on to her but there's not much escapes me round here. I reach out my hand, I put the coin in my pocket and just then there's a noise and it's the upstairs window lifting and Mrs Husting is leaning halfway out still in her nightgown with a shawl around her.

'Good morning, my dear,' calls out Mr Husting.

'Good morning, Mrs Husting,' I say. 'What a pleasure to see you. How are you on this bright sunny day?'

She gives me her usual look, which is to say the look she practises on me in case she opens her window one day and there's a pile of dead fish in her backyard.

'Sylvester. Did you give that boy a penny?'

'No, my love, I did not.'

'That shawl is very becoming on you, Mrs Husting,' I call up to her.

'Because we pay a fair wage straight to his mother, you know that.'

'I do know that, my pet.'

'A lovely shade of blue. It matches your eyes.'

'I'd like to know who else in this city would suffer to have the likes of him hanging around morning and night and pay for the privilege. Hundreds of boys wanting work in a two-mile radius, good boys, not layabouts. Boys that don't squander their opportunities.'

'I'm visiting the Shearers today. They're moving. They won't be needing their girl's bed now she's married. A set of chairs. A near to new Malvern Star and an old copper. I'm going past the shops.'

'Sherbet bombs and some jersey caramels. And don't be late tonight. I've got a nice piece of corned beef and Elsie's doing a cauliflower cheese. I dare say it's been some time since Jack's had a cauliflower cheese like Elsie's.'

'He was dead to the world when I walked past his room, just like he was still a boy,' says Mr Husting.

'He's tired from the travelling, that's all,' she says.

This past week I've scrubbed each brick in the yard and repainted the window sills and weeded the garden while Mrs Husting and Elsie cleaned every nook inside, on account of Jack coming home yesterday. This seems to me the greatest waste of time since the brothers made us clean the inkwells. If I was away from Ma and Connie for eighteen months I wouldn't notice if the garden was weeds from one end to the other. It's not only the Hustings, though: it seems like everywhere you look, people are moving, getting things ready, putting affairs in order.

Mrs Husting almost closes the window, and then she notices me again, Charlie's brush in one hand going numb from the cold, the other deep in my pocket squeezing the shilling. 'And can you get that one to scrub the dirt off that load of shovels without ruining them?'

'Dirt?' I say. 'That'd be the brownish stuff, would it?'

She gives me a look that could melt steel. It's a miracle G-men from America haven't parachuted in the street and carried her off because Mrs Husting could be a government secret weapon. If she turns her head an inch too far, that look would miss me and ignite the stables. Charlie snorts. Even he can feel it.

'I'll get him on to it when we get home from the afternoon run,' Mr Husting says.

'Just keep an eye on him,' she says. 'I know his sort.'

When she closes the window Mr Husting smiles at me again and taps the side of his nose with his finger. 'That shilling. Our little secret. Gentlemen's honour.' He holds out his hand, just like Dad used to do.

I hold out my hand and shake on it. I even say, 'Gentlemen's honour,' as well, just the way he said it. There's no excuse for that kind of dumb.

———————

Being known as chief *layabout and squanderer of opportunities* in all of Richmond is a big responsibility. Maybe it's those missing seven minutes. Maybe if Francis was the one who came seven minutes later everything would be different. I'd still be at school, for a start. But the fact is I followed him out so here I am, stable boy in charge of horse excrement transportation and shovel scrubbing at the Hustings'. I like it, mostly. Believe you me there's heaps of things about school I don't miss. Believe you me.

———————✦———————

The busier you are the faster the morning goes and in half a mo it's time for breakfast. That's the best bit of working next door: walk ten yards down the lane, around the corner to our back gate and like the Phantom, here I am at home. I didn't know how cold I was until I walked in. Connie's already at the stove and Francis is in his school shirt and tie having his cup of tea and there's the smell of bacon frying.

'Are your hands clean?' says Connie.

There's no point even answering on account of my reputation so I hold them out in front of me, nails up.

'Make sure, Connie,' says Francis, about to stick a piece of buttered toast in his gob. 'We don't want horse manure all over the kitchen. Maybe we should make him eat outside. As befits his station.'

Now I wish I'd given my hands more than just a quick one-two under the tap before I left the Hustings'. I can see a bit of something under my thumb nail that may or may not have derived from Charlie. Connie's not blind.

She picks up my hands and turns them over and then she looks at Francis. 'Perfect,' she says, and she kisses the top of my head. Then she gets another two rashers out of the icebox.

'Better check his hands too, Connie,' I say. 'On account of his head looks identical to his backside which causes all manner of confusion when he's on the dunny.'

This may not be the smartest thing to say considering our heads are near impossible to tell apart but anyway as soon as the words are out I hear a noise behind me and I know it's Ma. And sure enough there she is, in her black dress and white apron for going to work.

'What did you just say to Francis?' she says.

'It's all right, Ma,' says Francis. 'I'm used to it. I strive to be the bigger man.'

Ma narrows her eyes at me. 'We're halfway up the hill young man and you talk like we're still in the gutter. You'll keep until I get home. Don't think you're too big for the wooden spoon.' She sees Connie about to pop the rashers in. 'That bacon is for Francis and Mrs Keith.'

'Kip's been working since four,' says Connie.

'Francis needs meat in the morning, for his brain. Kip's lucky to be getting bread and dripping with his standard of behaviour.'

Connie puts the rashers back and gets the dripping from the icebox.

'Mrs Keith will have washing,' Ma says. 'And don't forget the tablecloths. And the iron is dirty. Clean it before you start. And iron both sides so the embroidery stands out.'

'I always do, don't I?' says Connie.

'And get Kip to cut some more wood. It's freezing in here,' says Francis. 'If he can fit it in around his other responsibilities of course.'

'Righto,' I say.

'I'd hate to overburden you,' he says. 'Only do as much as you can manage.'

I finish my bread and dripping and take the plate over.

'Don't want you working yourself into a state of nervous collapse,' Francis says.

'Shouldn't you be going?' says Connie.

'I've got ten minutes yet,' says Francis. 'Kid gloves, Connie, kid gloves. Don't let Kip's menial constitution fool you. He's a delicate flower at heart.'

'You're a good boy, thinking of your brother,' says Ma. 'Shame that knife only cuts one way. Shame not all boys appreciate a good education. Gladys told me she saw St Kevin's boys with their ties off in Bridge Road on Friday.'

'Disgraceful,' says Francis. 'I'll tell Brother Cusack.'

'I bet you will,' I say.

'Don't you take that tone, Christopher Luke Westaway,' Ma says. 'Francis is shouldering his responsibility, keeping his scholarship. Then he'll get another to the university to study the law as discussed. As it is we've had to take in Mrs Keith and I spend all day on hands and knees cleaning for other people when we ought to have a girl ourselves. Your sister giving up her art school. Your father, spinning like a top.'

'Don't worry, Ma,' says Francis. 'Aren't I the smart one?'

'That's my good boy,' says Ma.

10

'Anyway it's selection for the first eleven tomorrow. This year I'm a cert,' Francis says.

'Bradman must be shivering in his boots,' says Connie. She's prodding Francis's bacon with a wooden spoon. I can hear it sizzling and it smells like heaven. 'Cricket seems awful frivolous for someone destined for university.'

'That's a common misconception. One thing I've learned is this: all the best people play cricket. Being in the first eleven is an advantage for a fellow starting out in the world.' Francis picks up his knife and fork and throws his tie over his shoulder, ready to leap on the bacon as soon as it hits the plate.

'If the world stays as it is,' says Ma. 'That Mr Hitler. Heaven knows what he's capable of. Last time it was boys not much older than you that were going. Forging their mother's name and so forth. I'd sooner hide you in the ceiling space. I want you safe in school, not running around waiting for the call-up.'

'Don't be silly, Ma,' says Francis. 'The damn commos, they're the ones we ought keep an eye on. Them godless Ruskis. Jerry learned his lesson the last time. It'll come to nothing, everyone says.'

'That's how they speak at the university, is it?' says Ma. 'Language, Francis. How many times?'

Connie wipes her hands on her apron. 'Who's everyone?'

'*Everyone* everyone,' says Francis. 'Brother Marlow, Brother Rahill.'

Connie throws her head back and gives a little laugh. 'Oh I see, *everyone*. All the experts fresh from County Cork. Real men of the world.'

'Shows what you know. It's in the *Argus*. Mr Chamberlain, he'll have those continental types toeing the line quick smart. Even Mr Menzies says so.'

I don't know about Mr Chamberlain because gone are the days when I waited for Dad to come home so I could read his *Argus* and I've got nothing to say about Ruskis or damned commos or anything else. That's not my life, that's Francis's. All I know is every working boy in Richmond is waiting and watching. Half afraid war'll happen, half afraid it won't.

'Ma,' I say. 'I've been meaning to tell you. Mr Husting's going to have me in the shop any day now, I can tell. He'll get me a tie and an apron and teach me all about antiques.' Which isn't really a fib because I know he's going to. Didn't he just give me a shilling?

'It's not antiques,' says Francis. 'It's a junk shop, even Ma says.'

'It's not,' I say. 'It's house furnishers, china dealers and carting contractors. It says so on the front door.'

'Oh she'd love that, wouldn't she?' says Ma. 'Her ladyship Ada Husting. Wouldn't she love to have you inside to order around all day? Lord it over us now we've had a few turns of bad luck. What have I done? I've offended in the eyes of the Lord. There's no other explanation for how I've had to suffer.'

Attention jockeys, stewards and trainers: we're off and racing. Once the Suffering of my mother begins there's no stopping it. We all know to be quiet and not catch her eye. Even breathing can get you into strife. I sit still and keep my head down and chew. Connie puts the plate of bacon in front of Francis and turns her back and puts the kettle on the hob to start the dishes. Out of the corner of my eye I see Francis pick up a fat rasher, chomp it and roll his eyes, while Ma wipes her face on her apron and goes on and on.

———✦———

One of the jobs decreed as not too testing for we of the menial constitution is the fetching of the shopping. In the afternoon I go to the butcher's in Bridge Road for Connie. She gives me a list and without even looking I know it'll say a neck of mutton and more bacon for Francis and Mrs Keith. Perhaps some sausages. Ma won't stand for Connie giving me money so it all goes on the tick.

I like the butcher's. Butchering would be a good job. What does a butcher need with school? He needs to know good meat when he sees it, he needs to be strong and he needs to add up sums in pencil on the edge of the paper. Even I could manage that. You get a long blue-striped apron and a scabbard. It would be hard, some days: lifting the carcasses, sharpening the knives, scrubbing the tiles and the mincer and cleaning the windows, sweeping up the bloodied sawdust and laying down fresh. I like the colours here: the blue and white of the tiles, the red of the blood. Maybe I could start as a delivery boy. Maybe I could get a bicycle and carry meat and ham and loose eggs wrapped in paper inside string bags.

'Away with the pixies again?' The butcher raises an eyebrow.

'Righto.' I take the meat in its white paper and open the door and the bell tinkles like it's laughing at me.

It's late already. It's safest to be home before the tech school bell so I walk down Bridge Road and thread through the skint blokes standing on the footpath in front of the pub for the smell of the beer, and their smokes remind me of Dad and some give me a nod and a *how's the family Kip* and everyone's talking about the war that's coming that's a plot against the working man and I say hello and nod right back like working men do and I'm about to turn into Church Street to head home and I hear her before I see her, voice like the butcher's bell but sweeter. Of all the people to meet while carrying a bundle of stuffed pig innards. Why is she roaming around at this time of the afternoon? I throw myself into the door well of the draper's then crane my head around the corner and I catch a glimpse of shiny black shoes and thick black stockings and I know it's her. She's talking to someone at the top of the lane and how am I supposed to get home now? If I walk back the other way around the block I'll be late but if I walk on she'll see me and then what will I do?

So I wait and wait and after a while I can't hear her laughter anymore. I sneak my head out and she's not there and thank God for that so I walk into the lane and then all at once someone speaks and I jump out of my skin and drop the meat on the cobbles.

'Hello,' she says.

'Cripes.' I place my hand flat on my chest. 'A man wouldn't want a dicky ticker.' I pick up the meat and there's a bit of dirt on the paper but no one's going to notice. Extra tenderising, free service.

'You're Francis's brother, aren't you? I'm Annabel Crouch.'

14

I tell her I'm pleased to meet her and I manage not to laugh. *I'm Annabel Crouch*, she says, as if I haven't noticed her in church every Sunday since her and her father moved here. As if every boy for miles around that finds himself saying rosaries for unclean thoughts doesn't know who Annabel Crouch is.

'I know Francis from dance class.'

Dancing is something I never tried. Connie learned for a while, when she was still at school. Dad would put the wireless up loud and they'd go into the backyard because inside was too small for two people to turn and she'd teach him. Over to the vegie patch, down to the dunny, across to the tree and twirl. A pair of galahs, Ma said. The thought of Francis twirling is not at all attractive.

I tuck the meat under one arm. 'I imagine Francis would be quite a sight on the dancefloor.'

'He says it's an essential social skill for the modern young man. You look just like him. Only different. You're not at St Kevin's anymore, are you?'

'Me and school. I'd had enough, well and truly.'

'Shame. Heard you got the prize for English Composition. And Art, wasn't it?'

'Those days are well behind me. Being bossed around by brothers and prefects. I'm my own boss now. In a manner of speaking.'

'Francis is a very good dancer. He's good at all sporty things. And so thoughtful. He'd have been in the first eleven last year, except they wanted him to help with the coaching. To give the other kids a go. But you must know that already.'

I think of Francis at dance classes. New shoes, piano in

15

the corner, arm around Annabel Crouch. Tea and biscuits. 'Indeed. Nothing you can say about Francis is news to me.'

'And the way he knows all the serials from the radio,' she says. 'If you ask real nice, he does The Shadow so's you can hardly tell his version from the real thing. Must be good to have a brother.'

'Yep.' I move the parcel to the other arm. 'I can barely sleep for happiness.'

This talking to pretty girls business: who'd of thought it'd be so easy? Here I am, sausages and all, chatting away to Annabel Crouch like she's Connie. I stretch out one arm and lean against the wall, all casual, like I'm in a film. Things are looking sweet.

And then. Disaster. Annabel Crouch smiles. All at once something happens to my arm and my eyes and stomach and my Adam's apple. Her smile's got a direct line to her eyes and her heart. All at once I can't swallow so good. How did I swallow before, without thinking about it? My arm, the one leaning on the fence, is frozen with embarrassment. It doesn't know what it's doing stuck out at such an angle. I don't look like a film star, leaning here. I look like a one-armed man trying to keep a wall from collapsing without anyone noticing. Why am I trying to hold up a wall? Her lips, her teeth. Annabel Crouch probably gives away a hundred smiles a day, no charge, but this particular one is all for me. I can see behind her ear where the hair is pulled tight into her ponytail, the long white line where her skin joins her scalp, tiny soft yellow curls escaping. It's like a picture: the white of her skin, the yellow, the red brick of the building behind her. The way the sun bounces around the road, off the walls. I blink for a second, quick. To fix it in place.

'Are you walking back to Rowena Parade?' she says.

I nod. The arm on the wall, it doesn't feel like moving.

'Now?'

My stomach gives a flip. If I say yes, does that mean she'll want to walk with me? How will I manage not swallowing for the next five blocks? I'll drown in my own spit. And what if my legs forget how to be, like my arm has? I shake my head.

'Oh,' she says. 'Never mind.'

Then she waves, and she's gone before I can say anything clever that Annabel Crouch would remember in five minutes' time. I lean over, hands on my knees, and it takes me another five minutes to stop breathing in a pant.

She won't forget that in a hurry. Scintillated, she was. What is her father thinking, letting her walk around the streets anyway? If I had a daughter like that, a girl with Annabel's hair and Annabel's smile, the last thing I'd do is let her walk in lanes and talk to the likes of me. And I'd never let her dance with Francis, not on your nelly.

So before long my throat's remembered how to swallow of its own accord and now I'm thinking *what are you doing out of school early, Annabel* and *I love dancing, what is your favourite dance Annabel* and *I believe you're an only child, aren't you Annabel* and *Can I walk you home* and *Your hair is like fairy floss*. Bugger.

I own the lanes, mostly. I know the web of them, every lane in Richmond. I know which houses have a 'to let' sign on the front so they should be empty but there's a light at the back which means a two-up school's moved in. I know the corner on the other side of Coppin Street where you can peel back the corrugated iron and get at the Hagens' apricots. And down towards the river, the damp dog-leg where weeds grow as high as your hip and where the beetles meet in summer and you need to dodge the rusty tins and rabbits' guts and I know which cat rules the stretch behind the fisho where he throws the heads but would you believe it as I come into the lane across the other side of Lennox Street I'm thinking about Annabel Crouch and smack.

I walk straight into the four stooges, lounging on the corner like it's somebody's front room.

'Well, if it isn't Westaway Junior,' Mac says.

'Yeah,' says Cray.

So. The day has finally declared itself. It's peeled off one fancy leather glove, slapped me across the face with it and thrown it on the ground. Now I'm the one who's got to pick the ruddy thing up. On-bloody-guard, d'Artagnan.

'Hello, my little fish-eating friend,' says Jim Pike. 'Are you doing errands for your ma like a good cat lick? Tell you what. Just to show we're all friends here, all for the mighty Tiges, I'll give you a ha'penny to shine my shoes.'

'Hello Pike. I can see your shoes are a bit on the shabby side but no thanks all the same. I don't know where your ha'penny's been.'

We're in the widest part of the lane, with bits of corrugated iron on either side and bluestones sloping to a channel in the middle, filled with muddy water and other stuff that doesn't bear thinking about. Leaning against the fence is a boy I don't know. He's smoking, shirt pulled out of his pants and socks down, no jumper. The kind that won't let on when he's freezing. He throws his ciggie in a puddle and it hisses and smokes. He says, 'Who's this one when he's at home?'

'This, Manson my old pal, is one Kip the drip Westaway, the baby brother of Saint Francis,' Pike says. 'He's the most famous shit shoveller in all of Richmond. Straight from a cushy scholarship at St Mick's, suit and tie and pious expression, to his current position at the rear end of a horse. It's a wonder you haven't heard of him back in Sydney.'

'He cried when he left school. Like a weeping statue of the virgin,' says Mac.

I know crystal where they heard that from. 'As much as I'd love to stand around taking tea with you ladies, I have my own ha'pennies to earn.' I try to walk past them but Cray grabs me by one arm and Mac takes the other. The parcel of meat falls to the ground. Again. By the time I get home it's going to be mince.

'Actually,' says Pike. 'There's a job going where my dad is. On the line. You should pop your head in, Kipper.'

Mac shakes his head. 'A problem with that plan, Mr Pike.'

'Ah so,' says Pike. 'The notice says cattle ticks need not apply.'

Cray starts laughing.

'This is one of them boys?' says Manson. 'Master Mick MacMichael of Ballymicksville, eh?'

'Keep up, Sydney,' I say.

'Shall I tell you the story of Kip the drip?' says Pike. 'It's a long and sad tale that reminds me of a storybook. Who was

that writer? The old timer, Kipper? He was, I believe, a—
what you would call a proddy dog. English. Name escapes me.'

'That'd be Dickens,' I say. 'Nobhead.'

'Ah yes. Just like Grape Hexpectorations, our story starts
with the family in somewhat reduced circumstances on
account of the sudden demise of Kipper's old man. Who
dropped off the tram in Swan Street somewhat the worse for
a whisky or three and hit his head. Blam, splashed his brains
all over the read. A sad end.' Pike shows his teeth. 'Goodnight
Josephine.'

I can feel Mac's and Cray's sticky fingers pressing the flesh
of my arms. My heart's racing like it's going to pop through
my chest. I don't wriggle. I stand dead still.

'Those shortsighted men in full and gainful employment
who neglect to make provisions for their families in the case
of accidental death or dismemberment deserve what they get,'
says Mac, whose father is in insurance.

'Yeah,' says Cray.

'I see the elocution lessons are paying off, Cray,' I say. 'Any
day now you'll come out with a full sentence.'

'Funny,' says Cray.

'A bit of respect, Kipper.' Mac kicks the back of my calf
with a thick toecap. It'll come up in a beaut bruise tomorrow,
but right now it hurts like there won't be one. I turn my head
to the side and deliver a huge yawn into my shoulder.

'Sorry, sorry,' I say. 'Don't mind me. As well as a face only
a mother could love, you've got a real knack for storytelling.'

'With your permission, Fishface,' says Pike, but all at once
I am no longer here in the lane with these gorillas but back

in the kitchen those first days when I knew we would never see Dad again. I had been reading that morning before he left, sunk so deep in a book I barely looked up to see him go. His hat would've been pulled down over his ears like always, satchel in his hands, nails black from the ink, and when he rested his hand on the top of my head, I barely gave him the smallest glance before he went to work and then that night Ma crying, in shock the doctor said, and Connie red-eyed and running up and down the hall with tea and hot washers and tablets from the chemist's. I remember the edge of Dad's hat had some tiny black hairs stuck to the brim. The barber hadn't brushed him down properly. I thought we should buy him a new hat for the funeral because he wouldn't have liked to rest through eternity with those little hairs stuck there but I didn't dare ask Ma, her face was so white before his Mass, and now he's under the ground and it's much much too late.

Pike is smirking now and the new boy, Manson, spits a big gob right next to my boot with remarkable precision for such a hefty hoik, clear and frothy white. He smiles. By that I mean the corners of his mouth go up. Cray's fingers are hot on my arms and I have just one chance and I'm going to take it. No sense worrying about future repercussions if I'm not alive to enjoy them. I lean a little forward. On the bottom of Cray's chin, a few stray hairs are peeking through.

'Cray,' I say. 'You're holding me awful tight and awful close. Are you not getting enough cuddles off Mac these days?'

He lets go and pulls his arms back and jumps away and Mac does too. I kick the meat as hard as I can and it goes flying down the lane. The paper unravels and I scoop it up and I lose a sausage or two but I've gained a good twenty yards. 'Get him!' I hear.

But I'm Jesse Owens, I'm Jack Titus, I'm Decima Norman, excepting I'm not a girl. I fly out of the lane, pounding the cobbles like the Nazi hordes are hot behind me, across the road and they're breathing hard, and I'm around the Hustings' into our lane and I've taken the corner too sharp and down I go, bang crash, arse over T. My knee and elbow scrape on the bluestones and it stings like buggery but there's no time for that now, up again, in the back gate and bolt it behind me.

Five minutes later I'm still sitting on the step, head between my knees, gulping like a landed fish when Connie comes out of the back door. I see what she sees: dirty meat spilling out of the paper on the ground, me with a knee and an elbow dripping blood on the path, one side of my shorts and half my shirt wet with mud and filth.

She sits beside me and slides an arm around my shoulders and she's warm and she's Connie and I'd like to sit there forever being held like when I was little but I know I'd blub so instead I say it's nothing.

'Nothing, eh. How did this nothing happen?'

'I fell.' I look at the stitching on the side of my boot.

'I bet you did.' She doesn't ask anything more and I'm glad it's her that's found me, not Ma or Francis. She sticks out her hand and hauls me to my feet. 'Let's get you cleaned up.'

'Sorry about the meat.'

She screws her nose up but says, 'It'll scrub up all right and what they don't know won't hurt them. I can't, however, say the same for you.'

She helps me limp to the laundry then fetches a wet washer and some soap and that evil red stuff and I bite the inside of my lip while she pats and prods with tweezers and takes bits of gravel out of my knee and elbow and she's gentle and she talks about nothing, a dress she saw in a window and that Italian family in Tanner Street, and I know she's trying to take my mind off it like I'm a kid. I'm not a kid and soon I've had all I can take.

'Mr Husting's shovels,' I say.

Connie stands with her hands on her hips, looking at my knee. She's been cutting chokos off the back fence for tea and she's wearing an old dress of Ma's and her apron has green stains and her hair has fallen out of its bun and is across her face in black wisps.

She looks different now from when she went to art school. Tired. When me and Francis were little and she used to tuck us in, Connie's hands were soft and now they're rough. There's a red scaly bit across her knuckles. It looks itchy and sore. Her nails are all broken off.

'My medical opinion is: you'll live. I'll finish it after tea. Those stains should come out all right. Mrs Husting'll have a fit if she sees you like that. Leave your shorts and shirt in the trough and I'll soak them tonight.'

I do as she says and strip off and change and before I leave the yard I check. The lane is empty. They've gone back to Cray's mother's for sultana cake, the perfect little angels.

At the Hustings', I'm cleaning shovels and it's sweaty work and I put my hand in my pocket for my hanky and it isn't there which is strange, I took a clean one from the dresser this morning and Ma always says she'd rather we had no breakfast than no hanky.

Of course. These are new shorts. And then I remember. That shilling. It's in my dirty shorts, in the trough. It's not that I don't trust Connie, of course. But you never know about Francis. He's sworn to God but I've had things go missing from my pockets before: a cat's eye I'd only just won back when I was at school, two pieces of English toffee in foil and the bleached skull of a kitten I found half-buried down by the river. If I get one more shilling I could ask Annabel Crouch to come with me to the Glacerium, but if I don't get that one back right now I'll be kissing it goodbye forever.

When they put me in my grave, I know what it'll say on the stone, if I get a stone, if they don't bury me like a stray cat at the tip. *It was wanting to skate on ice with a girl that caused his so-called life to hit the skids.*

———+———

Hand on my heart, this is how it happens. I'm home early. Connie'll be calling me for tea any second and I need to get to the trough, quick, in case Francis comes nosing around. The sun drops fast these nights and it's nearly dark but I could find my way around the laundry blindfolded: roof tilting down on top of me, washing of clothes on the right and washing of Westaways on the left and I lean on the trough to find my shorts. The grey cement is rough and scratchy under my hands, mostly, with smooth patches already where Connie's rubbed the clothes on it. We bought the trough not long before Dad went. Ma was that proud. Lurking in the corner are the copper and the boiling stick and next to them an old tin bucket and the big brush. In the trough, there's a pile of dirty clothes and I find my shorts and pocket my shilling quick smart, and then I see a kind of silky dullish green almost the colour of the copper and I wonder what that is. When I untangle it from the rest and hold it up I see it's a pair of ladies' undies with white lace along the edges and by crikey, are they big. The bottom that fits these undies must be a bottom and a half. The queen, no, the empress of bottoms. The undies look funny, hanging there in the air by themselves without any lady in them, and I think about Francis at dancing classes and I wiggle the undies from side to side like a big dancing bottom. Then I think about the American parachutists coming for Mrs Husting and I throw them in the air to watch them fall, like being under a chute when it opens, and they drop down on my face.

That's when I see the light go on inside and hear the scream. A long, loud scream. I take the undies off my head. The kitchen bulb is swinging on its chain and the glow looks like a halo around her head and there in the doorway, Mrs Keith is holding her hands to the sides of her face like she's got a toothache, and she's screaming and screaming.

———✦———

Francis and me are lying on our tummies along the hall, just out of sight. There's been tea and hysterics and a fainting spell and a glass of sherry for medicinal purposes and all kinds of argy bargy. Connie's lit the fire, but still Francis and me have pulled the blankets off the bed and we're wrapped up like mummies, resting our heads on our hands, looking at each other.

Dad used to think it was funny to play like this when we were little. We'd face each other, move our arms, stick out our tongues, turn from side to side. Dad would say *ha!* and *do it again* and scratch his head and say *buggered if I know which one's the mirror!* But now I know. Francis is the real one and I'm the comic-book version. The one who shouldn't be allowed out by himself.

'You're dead,' says Francis. 'All over red rover.'

My tongue feels thick and my knee and hip still ache from when I came a cropper this arvo and my ear hurts from where Ma pulled me all the way to the bedroom. I feel like climbing out the window, jumping the fence and walking. I could leave and never come back, live like Huckleberry Finn, wild and without grownups.

'Sssh,' says Francis, even though I'm a mouse. We can hear them talking clear as anything. We'd have had Buckley's figuring out what was going on if we'd stayed in the bedroom with the door closed like we were told.

'Not one more night, not one more moment, will I stay under this roof. It's perversion, that's what it is. Disgusting. I should be calling the police.' I don't need to see Mrs Keith's face. I know she's sucking down her top teeth with her tongue until they are suspended halfway down her mouth then letting them go with a clack.

'Oh my Lord,' says Ma in a weedy voice.

26

'And for how long? His *face*. I can't even say it,' Mrs Keith says. 'I cannot even say it.'

'You said it all right this afternoon,' says Connie.

'My blessed Saviour,' says Ma.

'It turned my stomach,' Mrs Keith says. 'I had a distinct gurgling.'

'This is all over nothing,' says Connie. 'He's a boy. He was playing some game.'

'Wake up, girl,' says Mrs Keith. 'Menace all around us, abroad and right in this house. Wait until he's fully grown. He'll be a danger to decent women. He'll be strangling them in their beds. Dis*gust*ing, he is.'

'Cor,' whispers Francis. 'If you end up a strangler, we'll get in the *Argus*.'

'Keep talking,' I whisper back. 'The odds of me strangling get shorter with every word.'

'Strangler's brother tells all,' whispers Francis. 'My years of living with a maniac.'

'He is not disgusting. Ma. Tell her,' Connie says, from the kitchen.

'Story of survival against incredible odds. Courage and wit kept me alive, strangler's brother says. Letters from pretty girls pour in to handsome youth who shared bedroom with strangler his whole entire life,' whispers Francis. 'Photograph of handsome youth, page six.'

'Photograph of dead youth after his brother the strangler got to him, page seven,' I say.

For an instant, unless it's a trick of the light, Francis looks sorry. He leans towards me and pats me on the shoulder. 'The whole thing's dee-ranged. Why would anyone want some old lady's undies?' he whispers. 'You didn't really do it, did you?'

'Course not.'

'Then tell them what happened. Just tell them.'

I turn my head on the side and bump it against the floor. I think about Mr Husting's hand in mine. 'I can't. Gentlemen's honour.'

He rolls his eyes. 'You are an insult to cretins everywhere.'

I'm thinking what would be the worst that Ma could do to me if I'm caught out of my room and whether it's worth clocking Francis for when I hear Ma say, 'I don't know what to think.'

That can't be right. She's my ma. She knows what to think.

'See? Even your mother knows. He's a menace,' says Mrs Keith.

'I've had about enough of this, you old cow,' says Connie.

'Holy Moses,' says Francis. 'She'll have her mouth washed out for that.'

'What did you just call me, missy?' says Mrs Keith.

There's a noise—maybe a chair scraping along the floor.

'It's a good thing you're leaving,' says Connie, 'because you're not welcome in this house.'

'Please, please,' says Ma.

'Go on then,' Connie says. 'Good riddance.'

Me and Francis scarper to shut the bedroom door—well, as close to a scarper as I can manage while keeping my knee straight so it doesn't start bleeding again and my hip aching like it's been hit with a pile-driver and a whopper of a corkie on my calf courtesy of Mac and pulling the blankets behind us—and we shut it as soft as anything. We lean against it from the inside: me with my ear flat, Francis with his eye stuck to the keyhole.

Sure enough, in half a mo I hear Mrs Keith coming along the hall and slamming the door to her room next to ours. Everything is quiet then I hear another funny noise. I open the door and Francis is hissing at me to get down, that they'll see me but I don't bother. The noise is Ma, crying.

'You had no business speaking to her like that,' Ma says, between great gulps of air. 'We won't get another boarder in a hurry. Where will the money come from? Answer me that, Miss Smarty.'

Connie says nothing and that's the worst noise of all. For a long while there's quiet except a muffled stomping and slamming from Mrs Keith's room. Francis is telling me to get back but I walk down the hall and there they are in the kitchen, Ma sitting with her dress lifted up to her face, Connie on her knees beside her, holding her arms, cooing soft like Ma is a baby. They don't notice me at all.

'There's nothing for it,' Ma says. 'We can't live on my wages. Francis will have to leave school.'

I feel someone at my shoulder and it's Francis in my ear. 'If I have to leave school,' he says, 'I'll break every bone in your body.'

'No,' says Connie. 'I'll get a job. If we've no boarder there's no need for me to stay home. I can do the housework after I knock off.'

Ma lifts her head out of her skirts and wipes her eyes. 'And who'll give a girl like you a job, exactly. I begged your father to find you a good government job. It'd be more useful than drawing, I said. Something to fall back on. He wouldn't have a bar of it. Who'll give work to a *picture painter*?'

'I'll go in to the *Argus*, see some of Dad's friends,' Connie says. 'They said at the funeral. Gave us that lovely basket and said I should come and see them if there's anything they can do.'

I can see Ma and Connie looking at each other. I can see the outline of their faces, the parts that are the same, like the shape of their lips and their brows, and the things that are different, like the wrinkles around Ma's eyes.

'Shows what you know.' Ma sniffs. 'People say things like that at funerals. It makes them feel alive, like they can still do things, not like the poor bugger in the box. Words are cheap. I wouldn't give you tuppence for words.'

CHAPTER TWO

Stanzi

MY TWO O'CLOCK has daddy issues. She chooses the big red chair with the view of the park, not either of the simple black and chrome chairs opposite me. You don't have to be Freud to figure that out. She's cheating on her fifty-five-year-old husband with a man in his mid-sixties. And she's younger than I am. That, together with her eating disorder and history of kleptomania, gives us plenty of behavioural weaving to unpick. It's as if I was running a monthly special: three issues for the price of one.

'If I could remember my dreams,' she says. 'That would help, wouldn't it?' She's twirling in my red chair like an undernourished child on a swing. Her legs kick back and forth, back and forth. It's hypnotic.

Counsellors are not so interested in dreams. That's for psychiatrists with prescription rights and psychoanalysts with unconscious rights. She's been seeing me for over a year; surely she knows this.

'I'm wondering why you say that, Violet,' I say.

She doesn't answer right away; instead she curls up with her legs under her, naked feet rubbing against my leather. I can see her toes. Her pedicure is perfect, glossy peach moons sparkling, but it's the confidence with which she slipped her shoes off that's telling. She either doesn't know or doesn't care about the intimacy this assumes. Go on, Daddy's Girl. Make yourself at home. Someone else has to sit there tomorrow, but don't give it a moment's thought.

Against the bookcase my couch poses like a piece of installation art. That couch cost an absolute fortune. I bought it when I moved into this office more than ten years ago, when I was planning to do a PhD. Counsellors don't even use couches. I could have spent that money on a holiday. While I sit here on a Tuesday afternoon, listening to her, I could be recalling two weeks of sun-kissed splendour in the Maldives, where I would have drunk mojitos while a bronzed half-naked Maldivian called Omar massaged my feet. I was trying to do the right thing. Some clients would want to use a couch, I thought. Even if only ironically.

'Dreams are important,' Violet says, all innocent, like she hasn't just put me in my place. 'They're like my brain thinking while I'm asleep.'

'I can't argue with that.' I jot down her words, ready for the day I write my pseudonymous book about the things people say in counselling, the one that will make me a fortune so I can move to the Maldives and shack up with Omar. If the airlines ever get back to normal, if anyone ever flies again, if I haven't missed my chance forever. Outside it's a beautiful spring. The pink magnolias on the street outside are blushing to life. We should be cursing our hayfever and praying for Essendon to fight off the northern invaders at the MCG on Saturday, not wondering if the world will ever recover.

I blink a few times. Come on, Stanzi. Focus on why she's here, why she's paying me good money. 'Have you seen your father this week?'

'He took me to lunch yesterday.' Her individually articulated toes twitch like she's playing a tiny invisible piano, a sight I find creepy but mesmerising. Lunch with her father is like a date: she worries about her clothes, fusses over her hair, what to order, what he'll think of her. So much palaver just to eat.

'What were your thoughts about that?'

'He's too thin. Cheryl's not looking after him. My previous stepmother, Michelle—she was a better cook. Italian. All that pasta. At the time I thought she was making him fat.'

She thinks *he's* too thin? What is he, a Chupa Chup? Still, she's the one who brought up food. Encouraging this discussion is not a bad idea. 'What kind of pasta did she make?'

She stares at me like I've asked her the calorific value of snot. 'Do I look like Nigella Lawson? I don't know. Pasta. Different little shapes. With sauce on it.'

Right. 'And what did you and your father talk about over lunch?'

'This and that.' She swings her legs down and sits upright.

For a moment she looks very small, a tiny girl nestled in giant furniture. 'We talked about father stuff, mainly. What's your father like?'

'Mine?' She has taken me by surprise, something that rarely happens. I wouldn't have thought she was the type to be interested in anyone else's life. It's sweet, kind of. She may be realising there are other people in the world besides herself. Maybe that's why I answer.

'Funny. My dad's funny.' This is the short version, the *keeping communication channels open in both directions* answer. The long version would be this: my dad is a photographer, a great one. Art and commercial. He loves taking photos. And he's really smart. Mind you, he needs to be. He's one man alone in a femocracy. My mother, my sister and me: we throw our weight around.

'Funny huh,' she says, in a dull voice that tells me she couldn't care less if my father was the headline act at the Comedy Festival. Then she stands, bare toes wriggling into my thick-pile rug, and stretches her arms over her head like she's just woken up. 'Anyway. I spent Saturday morning shopping in Chapel Street. I've been picking up things again.'

This may not be the setback it seems. Sometimes problems can become worse for a while. Taking steps towards giving up a behaviour we define as part of ourselves can sometimes make us cling to it all the tighter. It's futile to fight your difficulties head-on. The only way to beat your unconscious is to sneak up on it. I'm reminded that even the very thought of dieting invariably leads to weight gain. Why? Say you make the decision mid-week, a Wednesday. When will the hypothetical diet begin? Monday morning. But that's four long days. Since we're starting on Monday, we might as well live it up today. One little bit of cake, a tiny slice of cheese, make the most of it. Regardless of what happens on Monday morning, the conscious decision never wins.

And besides, the way the world is lately. The tensions—it's enough to make cracks appear in anyone. The trick is discovering her personal pattern, her specific trigger.

'I'm wondering if there's something about that particular shop. Or something in it.'

'I doubt it. Nice things, of course. They're all idiots. They never catch me.' She smiles angelically and bats her eyelashes. 'They're looking for disaffected yoofs from the western suburbs. Losers. Not people like me.' She walks to the long window and looks out over the park. 'Sometimes,' she says, 'when I see a tower in the distance, I half expect to see a plane fly into it.'

From my office here in Hawthorn I can see the city, its skyscrapers huddled together like a slightly freaked-out forest. I know what she means. When I shut my eyes, I can see it also: over and over, from a variety of angles. Last week I saw a client who was planning a business trip to Sydney and mentioned it at dinner with her family. Her six-year-old became hysterical, crying and screaming and throwing things, clinging to her legs. When she calmed him down, she realised he thought every replay, every angle, was a separate plane spearing into a separate skyscraper. He thought all these hundreds of planes were crashing into buildings everywhere and his mother's Qantas flight from Tullamarine to Mascot would do the same.

'It's been a stressful couple of weeks for everyone, that's for sure,' I say. I speak slowly, make open hand gestures so she feels safe to jump in, to tell me how she feels. 'The way we see the world has changed for good. It's frightening. Lots of my clients are reporting an increase in their anxiety levels. Trouble sleeping, things like that.'

She rolls her eyes. 'They're wimps then, aren't they.' She abandons her shoes and walks the length of the room, pointing her toes like she's in *Swan Lake* and running her fingertips along my bookcase. She leaves flattened footprints in a silvery trail against the nap of the rug. 'I mean, it was stressful for the people who were actually *there*. We're on the other side of the world. Anyone who lives *here* and feels anxious is just a hysteric.'

'It's interesting that your shoplifting is increasing at the very time people are talking about a new war. A war in the Middle East. What are your thoughts about that?'

At the end of the bookcase, she rests her hand against the shelf while she does a plié. Her feet look alive, alert, like they're on her side. Then she shifts her weight and balances perfectly on just one. My feet are not on my side. My feet hate me. They ache to an extent I find impossible to describe, in every little bone and every cell of skin. They're uppity, my feet. They believe carrying me around all day is beneath them. Thanks to their bad attitudes, I have a cupboard full of shoes I can't wear and I even limp in these nanna-ish Mary Janes.

'That's just stupid,' Violet says. 'The Americans won't invade. It's the twenty-first century. Humans are no longer fodder for the military—industrial complex. We're evolved.

36

We are,' she pliés again, 'enlightened.'

'If there was a new war, would that concern you?' She was a teenager during the Gulf War. Me, I remember it clearly enough: sitting up all night, unable to believe this terrifying technicolour history unfolding on the screen.

She rolls her eyes. 'If they do invade, it'll take them six weeks max to fix up the whole Middle East. They're not the leaders of the free world for nothing. They're rolling in money and they're not stupid. I'm sure Bush has a plaque on his desk that says: *First rule of being commander-in-chief: do not fight a ground war in Asia.* If they go, they'll send the airforce to sort things out and be back in the officers' club for drinks at five. Everyone knows that.' She sounds so unlike her usual self I realise she's answered my question about what she and her father discussed at lunch. So now I say nothing. Silence encourages clients to fill the gap.

And she does. 'If there's anything we should worry about, it's SARS and people sending anthrax through the mail. That's what'll get us.'

'Is that a cause of concern for you? Opening things that come in the mail?'

'Of course.' She rubs her hands up and down her arms, like she's cold. She's not cold. If she was, she'd tell me to turn the heat up, pronto. 'You'd be an idiot not to be afraid of stuff like that. We're so fragile. We're like balloons filled with blood. The slightest injury, the smallest bug. Sometimes I feel we should walk around with our own invisible force field. Anything could do us in. There's malice everywhere. Don't you watch the news?'

37

The anonymous death, the one among thousands, the symbolic, representative, impersonal killings: she fears this not at all. She fears the deliberate, the targeted. Someone would need to aim for her. This is not a logical understanding of the risks, although I can see her point. If someone's trying to kill you, at least it should be about *you*.

She stops her circumnavigation in front of my desk. 'What's this?'

I know what she's asking right away. My desk is usually bare like every surface in my office, bare like every tabletop in my room. I like things sparse, lean, minimalist. Clutter makes my eyes ache. Charlotte and the kids, the mess drives me crazy.

Sometimes I put my foot down. When we moved in, Mum gave us a set of white lace doilies as a housewarming present. Doilies. They were wrapped in a striped linen tea towel with a wooden spoon holding the ribbon in place. So I can see where Charlotte gets it from. Our parents' place—God, it's a shrine to bric-a-brac shops the world over. It's where paintings of dogs playing poker go to die, every surface covered in shepherdess figurines and crystal koalas and miniature cars. And photos, of course. Newer ones of the kids and older ones of the three of us. Never Dad, because he's always taking the picture. It looks like my sister and I were brought up by a single mother with a time-delay camera. And there's no satisfaction in appealing to Dad. Despite his world-famous aesthetic sense and natural good taste, he won't say a word to Mum. He lets her do whatever she wants, he always has.

But today my desk is not bare. Today there is an old coin

on it, a shilling. I should have put it in the drawer with my handbag when I first came in. I don't know why I didn't. My theory of practice allows for some self-disclosure. An unguarded response can sometimes make clients feel safe, especially since it's Violet's relationship with her father that seems to be at the core of her troubles.

'It's my father's. One of his most prized possessions. Mum smuggled it out of his study. I'm getting it framed, as a get-well present from me and my sister.'

'Funny prized possession.'

'He says it reminds him of silver linings.'

'Money? That's a silver lining all right. I couldn't agree more.'

She couldn't be more wrong. It's just that he's attached to this coin. It'd be the first thing he'd grab if the house was burning down. He'd leave the art, Mum's jewellery, even his first editions.

'I'm wondering what your prized possessions are,' I say.

She doesn't answer. For the rest of the session, I try to bring her back to her father, her husband, her boyfriend, her habit of dropping things into pockets and open handbags. Instead she talks about a new nail bar that's opened in her neighbourhood, about trying to set her brother up with one of her friends, about someone she knew who left the window open while on holiday on the Peninsula and a duck flew in and shat on her friend's luggage, the bloody duck didn't care it was Louis Vuitton, so that night at dinner they all ordered the duck as revenge.

I don't know why she's telling me these things. I don't

know why she's here. More worrying is that I don't know why I'm here.

Eventually our time is up and I feel like I've felt for months now: like a child listening to the teacher drone on, then hearing the bell ring and knowing I can finally go home. My heart leaps; I can actually feel it, giving a little hop in its cage. This may be a tell-tale sign that all is not well on the career-satisfaction index.

Violet slips her shoes on and makes her appointment for next week. As we say goodbye she says, as she always does, *I feel better after our talk, Stanzi*. I wave as the lift doors close then hobble back to my office.

It's best to write up my notes now. I make a coffee in the communal kitchen amid the dirty mugs from the dental practice next door. I need some sugar to concentrate so I have a few biscuits from the packet in my desk drawer. Seeing Violet always makes me hungry. I've been in the game long enough to understand the power of suggestion.

Word association: Violet.

Crumble.

Where have all those biscuits gone? I went to the trouble yesterday to buy the ones with the cream filling, the revolting ones that taste like sweetened parmesan, in order to slow down their consumption and what has that achieved? I have struggled through an entire packet of cream biscuits I didn't like when I could have had cake. Sacrifice, without any reason or benefit. Life is too short for cream biscuits. I could be trapped in a collapsing skyscraper tomorrow and it would have all been a tragic waste of calories.

Today I have been productive. I've seen my usual assortment of middle-class, white, usually-but-not-always women with a giddying assortment of suburban problems that usually boil down to this one thing: *I've always been a good girl but the world has not kept its side of the bargain. When I was younger, I thought it'd be different. I thought something would happen. I would be richer, or prettier, or more famous, or more powerful.* Or (and this one seems exclusive to women), *I'm angry. I feel this rage come out of me and I'm so fucking angry I could break my fist through a wall. It can't be my family that makes me this furious. I love them. I live for them. But I don't know who else I could be angry at, or for what.*

They cannot keep the anger in, these women: they drink too much, they shoplift, they sleep with their doubles partners, they scream at their children, they pay someone to take a knife to their eyes or breasts or stomach. They turn the anger inward and develop a depression so deep they cannot get out of bed. The women come to my office and talk to me for a while and they feel better. And when they're talking to their friends and to their husbands they can say *my counsellor says*, so everyone knows it's not just them, it's not just some need to talk about *me me me*. It's a real problem and they have a real counsellor to prove it.

It's only later, when I ease my feet out of my Mary Janes and into my sneakers for the hike to the car, check my appointments for tomorrow and pack my handbag, that I notice my father's coin is missing.

———+———

As soon as I'm in the car, I dial Charlotte, quickly, before she leaves the shop and I have to wait until she cycles home to Rowena Parade. She refuses to carry a mobile in case the radiation kills off her brain cells. I suspect that ship has already sailed.

Some hippy answers the phone and, as usual, I wait, because in hippyland, as Einstein said, time is relative: Charlotte and I may have been born six minutes apart, but sometimes it feels like six years. She is with a customer or sweeping the floor with a broom made from free-range straw that died of natural causes or singing Kumbaya to the wheatgrass so it is karmically aligned. Finally, she's on the phone and, as carefully as I can manage, I ask her.

'You want to know *what*?'

I sigh. 'The year of the shilling. What was it?'

'Why do you want to know?'

'I'm considering doing a PhD on the random distribution of pre-war shillings in Melbourne suburbs.' The traffic is nightmarish. I dart around a car turning right and nearly sideswipe a truck. Times like these, I need a siren.

'Isn't it back from the framer's yet? They said they'd only take a week.'

'Yes. That's why I'm calling. Because it's back. It's in front of me. They've done a beautiful job. Polished wood trim, set in green velvet. Just like we discussed.'

'You haven't even taken it yet. Have you.'

At the lights, I look over to a bovine woman in the next car. She is staring straight ahead, chewing her cud, hair a colour unknown in nature. She doesn't notice me. When the lights change, she pulls in front of me with the oblivious insouciance of the entitled. 'Not as such,' I say.

In the background I can hear shop noises: the soft voices of calm people speaking, a knocking sound, metal sliding against metal. 'I told you I'd do it. I told you I'd cycle over in my lunch hour and pick it up and then ride over to the framer's.'

'And I told you it's easier if I did it. I have a fossil-fuel-burning vehicle and no regard for the level of pollution I generate.'

'If you haven't taken it to the framer's yet, you can just read the year on the shilling.'

There's nothing for it. I explain, almost accurately, about my difficult client and her predilection for nicking stuff and the trials of my life in general.

'I see,' she says, and I've known her my entire life so I know exactly what *I see* means. 'It's obvious what needs to be done.'

'What?' I pull over into a side street off Glenferrie Road, take the phone out of the clasp and press it to my ear. I brace myself.

'Violet is a troubled name. Bad feng shui. It's too close to "violent". She should change it. Maybe Viv, Viv's a nice name. Vivian. Sounds like vivacious. Then she can keep her initials. Except if her last name ends with an oh en. Vivian Morrison. Vivian Davidson. That wouldn't work. Vanessa would be OK. Another fun name. Risqué. Vanessa the undresser.'

'Wow. Thanks. Could we focus on the coin for now and leave the issue-solving to me? I'm trained. I'm the professional.'

'Are you absolutely sure she's taken it? It's not somewhere under your desk?'

I can feel my lips tighten, my eyes narrow. She means, *you've knocked it off the desk without noticing*. She thinks my spatial awareness is so poor that my brain doesn't know what my hip is doing. That I'm a bumbling, fumbling, bumper of shelves, an elbower of glasses, a jostler of knicknacks. Clumsy. I lean back on the headrest. I want a new car, with bench seats and fins and a wheel big enough to steer the *QEII*. Why is everything in my life so tiny and mean?

'Oh. My. God. You're right. As usual. It's fallen under my desk. I'm a complete idiot who doesn't even know if she's had a priceless family heirloom stolen out from under her nose. It's a miracle I'm still alive because with my IQ, I could have forgotten to breathe by now.' I contemplate putting on my hazard lights. *Warning! Approach driver at your own risk!* 'Do you know the year of the coin or don't you?'

'I still don't understand why you—' She shrieks like something bit her. 'Stanzi. Oh no.'

'Oh no, *what*?'

'You can't just replace it with another coin. It belongs to Dad. It's got to be that exact one.'

'Charlotte. It's just a coin. I'll find another one from the same year in one of those shops in Flinders Lane.' Silence. 'Charlotte? Charlie?'

'You will absolutely not be replacing it.'

For God's sake. How did I come to be related to the karma police? 'Look. He'll never know.'

'That's not the point. How can you not see that's not the point?'

'It's a unit of currency formerly in common circulation. It's

44

not the Ark of the Covenant. They made millions of them. Their own mothers couldn't tell them apart.'

Then she lands the killer blow. 'I'm very disappointed,' she says, and I can imagine the corners of her eyes drooping. Considering the 'very', her lips might have gone too.

'All right, all right. I'll go around to Vivian's place. Violet's. I'll get it back.'

'Stanzi. If it's a different coin, I'll know.'

After she hangs up, I sit for a moment with the phone warm in my hand. I imagine the soundwaves that have pumped through the air, threaded between the molecules of the metal of my car, vibrated along the street where they've joined up with more soundwaves from other phones that flood across the whole city, an invisible lattice, a web of messages. And what are these earth-shattering missives, enabled by squillions of dollars and countless hours spent developing this technology? *Do we have any pesto* and *I'm on the train* and *Don't forget to tape* Sex and the City.

I think back to when we were small, to our teenage years and our twenties. If anyone asks, I always say *this twin business in nonsense.* Or *if I had a psychic connection to my sister, believe me, I'd know—don't ask me how, I'd just know.* Or *you pronounced 'psychotic' wrong.* All those things she seemed to know: that time I broke my arm playing soccer and rang home and couldn't get Mum because she had taken Charlotte to the hospital with a mysterious pain in the same arm. Or that time at uni I'd broken up with the boy I thought was *the one*, and came home to find she'd stocked the freezer with five different flavours of ice-cream.

Coincidence and the power of suggestion, fairy stories for weak-minded people. A complete load of rubbish.

———✦———

The address in Violet's file is a flat in Kew—beige neo-Edwardian slash faux-Georgian with black wrought-iron gates and no eaves and ivy trained up the front wall. I've driven around the block twice but I can't get any closer so I park and scoff a tiny Mars Bar I found in the glove compartment. You need a magnifying glass and tweezers to eat a Mars Bar these days, thanks to those multi-national bastard companies and their cynical profit-mongering diminution of formerly normal-sized confectionery.

I had no choice. I had to come here. If I call and convince her to return the coin, I won't see it for another week. Dad will realise it's gone by then. Mum will smile and say, *Stanzi. Dear. Do you think you should have let Charlotte do it? We know how busy you are.* Which is Motherian for *your sister loves us more than you do, and what's more, you're a bad daughter.* Or maybe he already knows it's gone. Mum's hopeless with secrets. Or worse: the doctors are wrong and the pacemaker doesn't work. This won't be much of a get-well present if he doesn't last long enough to get it.

At the front door, I'm in luck. A pizza delivery guy has been buzzed in and he holds the door open so I don't have to declare myself over the intercom. We go up in the lift and all I can smell is pepperoni and melted cheese, oily and sharp and utterly compelling. Pizza smell is like radioactive waste: it's probably seeped into the fabric of my clothes and I'll have to dry-clean everything, otherwise every time I wear this outfit I'll be starving. It's after seven and I've had nothing but a banana and a skim latte, then a muffin at eleven. It's all right for mung-bean Charlotte. I have an efficient metabolism. Back in the cave, she would have been dead halfway through the first hard winter. The pizza guy gets out of the lift alive, with the box. He doesn't know how lucky he is.

I follow him along the tasteful corridor to Violet's apartment. Violet and pizza does not make sense. I hang back in a non-threatening manner and catch my breath but, when the door opens, it isn't her. It's a man in his early forties, short hair greying at the temples. He's in excellent shape; he stands the way fit people do, like their muscles could keep their body erect all by themselves, no bones required. I see sinews taut at the front of his throat. People who work out are so gullible. They think they'll live longer. Well, good luck to them. It's a shame most of them aren't bright enough to realise that the extra time added to their life when they're eighty and too old to do anything productive with it is roughly equal to all the time wasted in the gym when they're young and capable of having fun.

There's a quick pizza–cash exchange and, as the man says his thankyous, I lean forward and say, 'Excuse me.'

'Yes?' For a moment, his mouth considers smiling.

Can I have a slice? 'I'm looking for Violet Church. Perhaps I have the wrong address?'

He tells me she's not home and offers to take a message. I have seen Violet once a week for almost a year. This man is too young to be either the old husband or the older lover.

'Are you expecting her soon?'

'Are you a friend of hers?'

We could go on with this routine all night. Someone's got to give. He looks fit; he's holding that pizza box like it weighs nothing. I'm weak from hunger.

'My name is Stanzi Westaway. I need a quick chat with her. She knows me.'

The corners of his mouth turn down. He says my name, rolling it around in his mouth like he's learning a foreign language. 'You'd better come in,' he says.

I thank him, admire the hall, which is a different shade of beige, insist he begins his dinner. 'They're not as nice cold. The anchovies get extra furry. Don't let me stop you.'

He laughs, if you can call it that. 'This?' He raises the box. 'This isn't mine.'

He abandons it on the marble benchtop without even taking a peek inside, ushers me to the lounge and gestures to a two-seater the colour of oatmeal. Then, just as I sit, he says, 'What kind of name is Stanzi?'

'The regular kind. Short for Constance.'

He nods, as though my answer has given something away. 'Pays well, does it? Counselling?'

'I didn't catch your name.'

'I didn't throw it. Len Church. Violet's father.'

Well, well. Before I can reply, I hear the front door opening. 'Daddy?' Violet calls.

'In here, baby,' he says. 'You have a visitor.'

Violet has opted for the full Newton-John: pastel leotard, high ponytail and fuzzy wrist bands. When she sees me, she

48

drops her gym bag and it clatters on the parquetry. 'Oh,' she says. I say hello and wave. She does not wave back. Then she says, 'Did the pizza come?'

He points to the kitchen and we wait in silence while she disappears and comes back with four slices on a plate: two on the bottom, two upside down on the top. A pizza sandwich. I ask her if we could speak, in private.

Len narrows his eyes, settles further into his chair and rests his fingertips together like a Bond villain. Violet shrugs and sits on the wide arm of his chair, leaning back with her arm over his shoulder.

'I'll only tell him after you leave.'

'All right then,' I say. 'Good to know where we stand.'

I take a deep breath, and I tell them a gentle, circuitous story, one that cannot possibly offend, about how easy it is to drop things and how careless I am about putting things away in their right spot among all the things in my office, and how the coin is missing, the one I was showing her just hours ago. 'I thought you might have seen it. It might have fallen into your bag, or your pocket. I could have accidentally knocked it off the desk. It's my father's. It's very important.'

Violet stares at me, eyes wide like a skinny muppet. For the astonishment on her face I might be speaking Urdu. *That's it*, I think for a second. That blank look is an admission, of sorts. Shock that she's been caught and confronted after all this time, after all these stolen objects. A confession. Then she snorts and laughs and covers her face with her hand.

'As if I'd steal something so lame. A dirty old coin. What's it worth? Nothing.'

'I wasn't implying anything.'

'You should know I'm a lawyer,' Len says.

'Of course you are,' I say.

Violet sniggers at the thought of her avarice and skill spent on such silliness and all at once I know the coin is not here, not in Violet's bag or pocket or secreted in her bra. It's back in my office, on the floor under my desk, edge-downward in the deep-pile rug. It is exactly where Charlotte said it would be.

'I'm sorry to have wasted your time.' I stand, hand on my bag.

Violet and Len do not stand. 'Darling.' He takes her hand and folds his fingers around her talons. 'I'm happy that you're talking to someone. I'll pay for anything you want. But can you honestly tell me it's helping, seeing this woman?'

'It does help.' Violet smiles up at me conspiratorially. 'It does. Every time I see her, I feel so much better. She makes me feel so grateful.'

I feel a rush of warmth for the scrawny little thing. I've come here, ready to accuse her of nicking something, of violating our counsellor–client relationship and she's defending me to her plastic father. I could almost hug her.

'Thank you, Violet. That means a lot to me.'

'It's true. Every time I see Stanzi, I think to myself: no matter what troubles I have, what else is going on in my life.' She smiles, and it's the sweetest, warmest smile I've ever seen. And then she says, 'At least I'm not fat.'

And I am captured, standing here, a smiling giant statue of myself carved from granite, massive hand on my bag, huge legs, half-astride, atop bulbous feet as if I was about to walk to the door. Back when I could walk. Even my face is petrified. It is a carving of wood that turned to stone long ago. It retains the appearance of a warm smile but the muscles are destined to remain like this for eternity.

Violet stands. 'I'll show you out.' Then she notices the plate of pizza on the coffee table. She flips the top piece over so its guts are exposed. 'I always order too much. I just feel bad for the driver, you know, coming all this way to deliver a small pizza. It doesn't seem worth his while.'

On top of the pizza, the cheese has congealed. The salami is round, shiny and prettily pink. It could be jewellery. The tomato looks like rust. All at once, I am amazed that this is considered food at all.

She smiles at me. 'Would you like to take it with you? It's a shame to waste food, don't you think? Go on. Take it. It'll only go in the bin.'

I am sitting in my mother's kitchen in Malvern. I have a vague recollection of saying my goodbyes, of driving here. I can only hope I did not cry before the door shut behind me. I think it's possible I called her Vivian.

I drove back to my office and knelt on the rug beside my desk—hold the chair, steady now, first one knee, then the other—and threaded my fingers through the pile until I found the coin. It is in my fist, in my pocket, sweaty and sticking to my fingers. I don't know how long I sat on the rug before hoisting myself up, but I am here now. It is late. My mother's kitchen is wallpapered in orange baskets of fruit: orange oranges and orange pears and orange grapes on a psychedelic orange background. She has made me tea with lemon, strong and sweet. Staring at me from the kitchen bench is a photo of me and Charlotte in our late teens, arms around each other, grinning. I'm not huge but there's a roundness in my cheeks and throat that marks my future. Charlotte looks the same as she does now. She's wearing Mum's amethyst pendant, so the photo must have been after our eighteenth birthday. I wriggle. These chairs are uncomfortable despite the padding. My thighs hang over the side.

'Would you rather something else?' Mum is wearing her dressing-gown, the one with the satin cuffs that I bought her. It's pulled tight around her slender waist and tied with a bow. Her hair is thin, that special shade of little-old-lady lilac. I am holding her tea cup in my mitt; one squeeze of my paw and it would shatter. The china is eggshell-thin, almost translucent, and old. So old I wonder how many people have held it as I am, how many lips have pressed against it just where mine would be. Kisses from strangers, transmitted by porcelain from afar. I lift the cup and lean it against my forehead, then my cheeks, and the heat seems to soften the hard pain in my head. It's late, I know. She was already in her dressing-gown when she opened the door. I should let her get to sleep.

'Mum,' I say.

'Are you hungry? Do you want something to eat? Toast. I could cut you up an apple. There's pumpkin soup in the freezer. It's five minutes on defrost. Five minutes.'

I shake my head and she waits, in that way she does. She

sips her tea and looks nowhere, as if she's looking for nothing, as if everything she's ever wanted is within reach and there's nothing to search for, nothing to do. The photographs of us are framed on the walls, the kitchen bench, on top of the buffet. In her youth she had a luminous perfection that radiates even from the old photos, the black and whites of her on her own. And that smile! Even now when she smiles, there's no one else in the whole world but you and it's impossible not to smile back.

Now her beaming face is a little shrivelled apple, red cheeks, all faux-indignation and a sly lopsided smile. In the right light, she'd pass for her mid-fifties. She's had a charmed life. Only child brought up by her father who died just before she married, a saint of a man who adored her. Dad was her first boyfriend and only love; she went from being looked after by one man straight to the bed of another. When you're beautiful, life is easy. Someone will always look after you.

The door swings open. 'Stanzi!' says Dad. He's in his pyjamas, an old-fashioned blue stripe, required bedtime uniform for the stylish elderly. During the day, he still looks sprightly, *not a day over seventy-five* as he says, but now he seems fragile and vulnerable, almost like a small boy waiting to be tucked in. Just the sight of him, my heart flutters on a string.

'I didn't hear you come in. How are you, sweetheart? Stanzi?' he says. Not *have you been crying* or *do you have any idea how late it is* or *you're not upsetting your mother are you?* He bends to wrap an arm around my shoulder, and he kisses me. My father kisses hello and goodbye. Friends, family and random strangers. I don't move. I can feel his warmth and bones and sinews through the flannelette. I don't even lift my

huge arm to touch his hand. I want to tell him I'm good, I'm
fine. I look at Mum.

'Good night,' Mum says.

'What?' he says. 'Why?'

'Later,' Mum says.

'Have I done something? I can undo it. Or if I haven't
done anything, I can. Just watch me.'

'It's nothing, Dad.'

'I can help, whatever the nothing is,' he says. 'I'm an expert
at nothing. Whenever anyone wants help with nothing, they
call me.'

'Kip,' Mum says. 'See you in the morning.'

'Secret women's business, is it? Just pretend I'm a girl.
A somewhat hairy girl.'

'Good night, Dad.'

'That's so unfair. It's discrimination, plain and simple,'
he says.

Normally he would stay and tease us more, this old joke
of his. When we were little, Charlotte and I loved it when he
sat on the floor with us, playing dolls or dressups. *Just because
I'm a boy doesn't mean I wouldn't make a fine girl*, he would
say, and we would laugh at our ridiculous father, so unlike the
fathers of our friends. Dad is not the least bit feminine and of
course that was the joke of it—this big man, nose bent from
a break that hadn't set right, folded on the floor, huge boots
and wide cuffs, nestling down with us. His big hands dressing small dolls, rocking one to sleep, brushing another's hair.
But tonight is not the time to play. He glances at my mother's
face and gives up.

'I'll say goodnight then, my beautiful girls.'

There is something in the way he says it. He sees me, but still he says it. I look around at the photos: at all the Alecs and Libbys, the Mums, Charlottes and me. 'I'm not beautiful,' I say. 'Mum and Charlotte are, but I'm not.'

He follows my eyes. 'Fifty years of family photos, but none of Connie. If you had met her, you'd see. You look like her. Beautiful.'

He kisses the top of my head, then shuffles back down the hall. Mum and I sit in silence a little longer until it comes out of me, I don't know where from.

'It shouldn't matter what I look like. What difference should it make? It's not who I am. Why should I care what people think? Why should I look like everyone else?'

'Of course it's who you are. It's your body, Stanzi, not anybody else's. So it is part of who you are. It has to be.'

'I don't feel like this on the inside.'

She pours herself more tea. Her eyes are a washed-out blue. I know her eyes. They've been looking at me my whole life. There's no hiding from them.

'That's a shame,' she says. 'The very least we can hope for is to recognise ourselves.'

'I can hardly walk up a flight of stairs. My thighs bleed from chafing. My feet hurt. All the time.'

'I know.' She leans forward and picks a bit of fluff from my jacket. 'Was someone mean to you?'

All I can manage is a nod.

'Was it someone you care about? Someone whose opinion matters to you?'

I think about Lolita-Barbie, her pointy little nose, her pointy little mind, her stretched-face father. 'No,' I say. 'It was no one I care about.'

'A girl, was it? A mean girl. Right.' She pushes up the sleeves of her dressing-gown in a dramatic fashion and waves her tiny fist in front of my face. 'I'm going to get in the car and drive to their house and walk up to their front door and ring their bell and they're going to get it from me. Them, and their no-good parents. Some people are badly brought up, that's all. Wait till I get my keys.'

I smile. I can't help it. When I was little I loved sitting on her lap, my face buried in her neck, her arms around me. Some nights it was the only way I could get to sleep. She smelled of baby power and raw onions. I'd love to nestle there now but if I sat on her lap I'd put her in intensive care.

'I'm thirty-five. You can't sort out the parents of everyone who's mean to me.'

'Why not? Why can't I? I remember Sharon Lisette, when you were in grade three. She was awful to Charlotte too. Charlotte the scarlet harlot, she called her. What did she say to you? Con Con smells like a tampon, was it? I spoke to her father about her filthy mouth. You're never too old to be someone's child. And if I get no satisfaction from those rotten parents I'll go all the way to their headmaster.'

'Small flaw in your plan. I don't have a teacher anymore. Or a headmaster.'

'I have a better idea anyway. I'll get your father to work her over.'

'He's seventy-six.'

'If he had the element of surprise—who knows? He could kick her in the shins and hobble away.'

It's an appealing offer. I tell her I'll keep it in mind.

Charlotte and I were born to two people who plainly adored each other. I was a teenager when I realised what a curse this was. It means I will never have a marriage like that. It will be impossible to find someone who loves me that much, ridiculous to think that lightning could strike twice in the same family.

And after all, what are my options? I know there are men out there who like a full-figured girl. I know there are fetishists and feeders, people who'd delight in my crevices and curves. Yet I don't want anyone who loves me only for my body any more than I want someone who loves me in spite of it. And the acid test of my acceptance and self-esteem, my one shot at authentic living? The truth is, fat men turn me off.

Mum strokes my hand. 'Are you sure about the soup? You always feel better when you eat something.'

Hot in my fist is the thing that's caused me all this trouble. I turn it over in my palm and my fingers brush against Mum's.

Maybe lightning isn't the best analogy for love. Maybe love is more like a coin: moving between people all around us, all the time, linking people within families and on the other side of the world, across oceans. If we drew the path of a single coin, the trajectory it had taken, it would link us to all kinds of strangers. We would be connected to people we've never even met.

'A shortbread? No?'

Fuck, fuck, fuck. All at once I see it.

It was not Violet who was responsible for the violation of our relationship. It was me. I have crossed the line. Going to Violet's home means I have put my own needs above the client's. A major professional transgression. I can't do this job anymore. Not for one more day.

There's a draught in my mother's kitchen, a window left open. The skin on my arm is puckered under my fingertips. I shiver: little goosebumps, a ghost walking over my grave.

'It's later than I thought,' I say. 'It's time I got moving.'

CHAPTER THREE

Jack

WHEN I WAKE a couple of hours later my head is wedged between the wall and the mattress. My feet hang over the edge. The spare pillow has dislodged during the night and the cast-iron rung is cold and hard against my calf. I am used to sleeping in my swag or a bunk but this bed is only just broader than my shoulders. One turn too wide or too fast—if I dream I am back among the horses and the sheep, cutting and weaving across the paddock—I'll be over the edge and face down on the lino. Way over on the other side of the room, three feet at least, the tiny chair is covered with my clothes. At least it's good for something. It'd never hold my weight and my knees wouldn't fit in that little space under the desk.

I've been home for months now, and they've a shop full of beds and mattresses and chairs downstairs. Furniture the right size could be up here in two shakes. Yet they don't mention it. It seems I'm the only one who notices I've grown. And I don't say anything either. This Gulliver life fits my mood, a stranger in a strange land.

There's a rap at the door. 'Jack,' she says. 'Are you awake?'

I can imagine her face close to the keyhole. She's been pacing up and down the hall for the best part of ten minutes. She's imagining what she might be disturbing. She is unsure how to mother a grown man.

'Yep.' Soft, but she'll hear me.

'I know it's a Sunday, dear. But we don't tend to lie in so long. Not normally.'

Sunday or no, every morning since I've been home she's knocked around seven and said *we don't tend to lie in so long*. She thinks me content to sleep half my life away in this little-boy room. She's concerned I've developed lazy habits, despite the work I do in the shop, lifting furniture, cleaning and repairing the whole day long. She doesn't know me. Not at all.

'Jack? You'll be coming to church with us?' she says.

Mum and Dad hadn't seen the inside of a church since my christening but that all changed when the King asked for prayers for the Empire, prayers that we'd defeat Germany good and quick. Since then, they've been every week and they're not alone: St Stephen's is packed to the doors. Another thing about this city I don't understand. If the power of prayer is strong enough to keep Hitler at bay, it should have come in handy before now.

'Not today,' I say to the door. Her footsteps fade.

There is no air in here. The window is nailed shut. When I went down to get a hammer to pull the nails out that first night, Mum said, *No Jack, please don't.* Her face screwed into a mess of wrinkles. She looked just like my mother, except older. *What with all the valuables we have downstairs and I've heard of burglars letting themselves in first-floor windows.* So that was that.

It's not just this room, not just this house. Even the sky's too low. The view is not the sunlit plains extended. Our part of Richmond, here on the hill, is an island. I can see over the roofs of the rest of it, mismatched shingle and rusty tin held down by lumps of rock and brick and jerry cans. A poor man's paddock, an endless field of patchwork. Palings missing from every other fence, taken for fuel last winter or the one before and never replaced. Advertising hoardings on every corner so a man can't even think his own thoughts without interruption. The barrenness, the ugliness, the sad crushed spaces.

For the life of me, I cannot see why people stay here. Do they not know what's beyond the city? A few hours on the train and their chests would fill with pure air, their shoulders would settle, their hearts would open.

The neighbourhood is stirring. A handful of trees struggle against the grey bitumen, limp in the shimmering heat.

Across the lane, in the tiny yard next door, I see a girl. She is wearing an apron, weeding the vegetable garden. She kneels, first leaning forward to pluck something from the soil, now leaning back, weight resting in the hollow of her joined feet. She stands and picks up the watering can, stretches to reach the runner beans on the far fence. She is dark-haired, slender and pale, a sapling bent with the weight of the water. She lifts it. The water arcs out and her body straightens. When the watering is done, she begins digging up potatoes with a garden fork. It's a miracle anything grows in this mean soil, heavy with factory smoke and flecked with rubbish. She rubs each potato between her palms as if she's spinning wool or making fire with a stick. When it's cleaned to her satisfaction she slips the potato in the pocket of her apron.

The girl is Connie Westaway. We used to play together before I went away to school. Her brothers are too young to sign up and Kip is day labour for Dad, an act of charity on my parents' part. I hardly remember Connie Westaway at all.

Now she is brushing her hands on the apron. Now she has picked up the broom leaning on the back wall of the house and she is sweeping the path that leads to the incinerator. I have finished dressing. I should go downstairs. Mum will have breakfast ready, or worse: she'll be standing beside the stove waiting for my order, as though there was a typed menu on the kitchen table. But here I am, hands on the sill, watching the neighbours' backyard. Connie moves her feet as she sweeps: a one-two sideways swish.

Now she stops. Is she talking to the broom? She holds it loosely between her looped thumb and forefinger while the other hand flutters at her chest. From this angle I can just make it out: she smiles. She curtsies. Honest to God, the girl just curtsied to a broom, as though she's at a ball or in the pages of an old novel. I wish I had a telescope. I cup my eyes with my hands to see her better. Now she places her other hand near the top of the broom handle and raises her eyes to the tip.

Bugger me dead. She is dancing.

One foot forward, then the other. Foot to the side, then the other, skipping to the fence, then back to the vegetable patch, one hand on the broom, the other holding her skirt. Now she twirls, skirt splaying out, a breeze of her own making. Around the post of the clothes line, back the other way. There is a young lilly pilly a few feet from the fence in the corner closest to our place: she is dancing around it and running her hands against the smooth trunk. Standing there in my bedroom, palms flat against the pane, I can somehow feel the bark on my skin. She dances back and I can see her feet, alive in small black boots. I can almost hear the music from the way she moves, as though there was a twelve-piece orchestra behind the fence. The piano cadenza as she bends at the waist, now a rising chorus of strings. The music is in my veins as I watch her dance, the rocking of her body, the turn of her white neck.

Then I notice: I am also swaying. If I had more than six inches of clearance I'd break into a jig. She has the joy of the morning in her, as if she's the only person in Melbourne who even knows it's a new day. Hours could pass and I'd still be watching Connie Westaway dance. She circles the backyard, once, twice, thrice, faster and faster. She is the loveliest thing I've seen in all these weeks I've been away from the bush.

She stops. The broom falls from her hand to the path—I imagine its clatter, wood on bricks. Mrs Westaway has come outside, talking fast, arms folded, head snapping from side to side. Connie walks in to the house, fast but not running, eyes ahead, not down. The broom she leaves where it falls. Her mother walks in behind her. The music has finished.

Another knock and this time Mum opens the door. 'Jack. What are you doing at the window?' She comes in and stands beside me, looks down, then back at my face. 'Your father's already eaten. What is it you'd like for breakfast? I thought you'd fallen back asleep.'

'Coming,' is what I say. But maybe she was right and I had fallen asleep. Maybe I was dreaming.

———

I have had many different sets of parents and lived in many different houses. This is something only my mates from boarding school understand. Fact is, everyone changes a little bit, all the time. We age and shrink and grow and soften and harden. When you see someone every day the changes smooth out, like when a young dog takes on a mob of sheep all by itself and you can't remember the exact moment it stopped being a pup. But when you're away, the changes aren't smooth. When you come home from school after five months or from working on a station after nearly eighteen—it's like different people in place of Mum and Dad.

This visit, the old man can't raise his arm above shoulder height because something went bung in the joint when he lifted a table funny last summer. Mum's different too. She sniffs the air now, when she's talking about other people. The women who were always over for tea, knitting on their laps, the last time I was here. Not hide nor hair of them now.

Both these things, the shoulder and the missing friends, they add up to something. Put together with the way they both puff while they're walking up the stairs, the way Dad looks for his glasses when they're perched on his head. Mum standing in the laundry, squinting at the socks, holding them up to the light after she's taken them off the line and still every other pair rolled in a ball in my drawer doesn't match. One black, one navy. One with a stripe near the top, one an inch shorter. I've told her I'll pair up my own socks, and I smile when I say it, but still it wounds her out of all proportion.

For of course we're not really talking about laundry. We are talking about them growing old without family around. They think I shouldn't have been so far away, working out west, even though it was them who sent me in the first place. With the war, they can hardly find able bodies for the shop. I'm only meant to be here for a visit but now that I'm back, I should stay.

Out on the station, everything's the same as it's always been. The hills and trees and rocks. There's always a kookaburra on the same branch, fish in the same bend of the river. Every time I come back to this house, it's a different world.

———————

Sunday grinds forward. I chop some wood, clean my boots. I see sparrows in the yard: loathesome birds on a farm but still living, wild things. I watch them fly and I think good on them.

Go, you little brown buggers. I don't think of music or brooms or the way a skirt twirls. The movements of dancing ankles.

By midday Mum's been watching my every move for four hours so I tell her I'm off out for a bit. I walk to Bridge Road and in the reserve behind the town hall there must be over a hundred blokes just standing around, smoking or cadging ciggies, having a yarn. There's a fellow in a sharp suit walking around selling raffle tickets but you'd have to be a real bushie to buy one. Someone has a football and there are jackets and hats slung on the fence while a mob of them run around kicking and handballing. The fellow with the ball goes down under a pack and the ones on top of him can hardly breathe for laughing. Silly buggers.

I take my coat off and fold it over my arm. There's not a lick of breeze and not enough trees for everyone to stand under. On the side of the oval, one of the stalls has penny pies and there's a crowd gathering, brought close by the smell. I feel in my pocket for some coins but it's too hot for pies. I can hear the talk around me: shrill, about the war. *Just because nothing's happening yet don't mean it won't*, says one. *Anything'd be better than hanging around here*, says another. Before Mr Menzies declared us to be behind England boots and all, it seemed men were squaring off: one lot for love of Empire, the other believing we should only fight our own battles. Now that's all changed—or else the doubters are smart enough to keep their mouths shut.

I can see both sides. I'm not like these boys who think it's a jape, who are busting to go. I've seen death at close quarters. A stockman crushed against the rail of the holding yard by

66

an unbroken horse. That shearer who drank himself blind on turps and walked into the fire, camp women dead in childbirth or kicked to death by husbands. I've listened to the sound of dry clods hitting a thin wooden box and I've seen the ever after coming for me, too. I've known that split second where everything stops and you think: *this is it*. There's a scar on my forehead at the hairline where a pick-head flew off and nearly lifted my scalp. It's only luck I'm still here.

All the same I can see why young blokes are more excited than scared by the thought of war. That mob standing under the tree; they're making plans to farewell mothers and fathers and girls. Nudging each other, laughing. I can see through their eyes the wonder in it, the thrill, pitting your luck against the horizon and never believing you could fall out the loser. Their big chance to see European stars.

The short hairs at the back of my neck tell me there's a bloke close behind me, maybe more than one. I don't turn. Then I feel a jostle, the bump of a shoulder against my arm. Two old men, one behind the other. The front one mutters something. There are flecks of white spittle in his beard. His hair is plastered flat with sweat. You can't find a pub open on a Sunday but I can smell his breath: malty and sour, old beer.

'I said, "And you, boyo".' His voice is a low bellow. 'Why are you still in civvies?'

The men around me waiting for pies hush as he speaks.

'Against the law, is it?'

'Against my law,' says the old timer. He puts his shoulders back and speaks like he's doing me a favour at great personal expense. 'I was at Pozières, young man.'

If I had any sense I'd turn and head home. Instead I say, 'And you'd wish that on another living soul.'

The man behind him has wet eyes peering out of speckled white skin. 'I'm half deaf, they say. I've been down the drill hall twice and they sent me home both times.' He cups his ear for effect. 'The question my old friend asked was: what's the matter with you?'

'He looks fit enough, doesn't he?' says the old timer. He walks around me in a circle. 'Tall. Broad. Nothing wrong with him, I'd say.'

'Strong as an ox and almost as smart,' says the second man.

If I had nothing to be ashamed of, I'd tell them about my parents getting older and worrying and how I have to help them. The look in my mother's eyes when she hears about another boy from the neighbourhood signing up. That if I was going anywhere it'd be back out west to the station, back where I can breathe. I'd tell them I haven't made up my mind to go. Not yet. But I say nothing.

'First soldiers are already there. Saw it in the *Herald*,' the first man says.

'Perhaps you think you're too good to go,' says the other.

'Perhaps I think my reasons are my business.'

'Now, now,' he says. 'Don't be like that. We're just offering a little encouragement to blokes who might be lacking in the spine department.'

'Them spineless blokes,' says the old timer.

'Hard to tell which blokes have nothing but jelly where their spine should be.' He waves a fly off the front of his face.

I take off my hat and hit it against my thigh to shake

the dust off it. 'I'll be sure and tell them, if I see any. Blokes without spines. I'll tell them you're looking for them.'

'You do that,' the younger one says. Neither of them moves. They just watch me go.

———+———

At home, Mum's picking up a load of fabric scraps from the kitchen table, red and white check against the polished timber. She sorts the bits that are big enough for patches from those to be thrown away, she gathers up her threads and needles. Then she starts bustling around the kitchen and I see the good cups being wiped with a tea towel and cake plates and forks out on the sideboard.

'Jack,' she says, when she sees me in the doorway. 'Why are you wearing that old thing? I've ironed your new shirt. How about putting it on?'

She wants me to wear the new shirt she bought from the Myer Emporium for Christmas. Now, for afternoon tea with her and Dad. This from my mother who, after twenty-odd years of marriage, takes the linen from her glory box twice a year to replace the mothballs. I don't say anything. I go up to my bedroom where the blue shirt is hanging on the door and I put it on.

When I get back to the kitchen she adjusts my collar. 'Look at the state of you. Did you shave this morning? We're not out in the sticks now, you know. How about running a wet washer around your neck? There's a cake of Sunlight in the trough. Go on.'

I sniff under my arms. Nothing I can detect. It's the first time she's asked me to do this in six weeks but if that's what she wants. When I get back, the kitchen is empty. I hear a murmur from the front room, Mum's company voice, higher pitched, with tighter vowels. I wander down the hall and she's sitting there with Dad and a woman and a girl, a brown-haired girl. The girl is wearing a red suit and a white shirt and her face is shiny and her hair is done up with a red ribbon. They all stand when I come in. Her teeth are straight and friendly. Good, strong teeth. There's not one thing wrong with the look of her.

'Jack,' says Mum. 'There you are. We wondered where you'd got to. This is Mrs Stewart and her Emily.'

Mrs Stewart nods. Emily steps forward and I shake her hand. Her grip is cool and firm. A proper handshake, not a ladylike drape of the fingertips.

'The Stewarts go to St Stephen's,' Mum says.

'Don't see you there, Jack,' says Mrs Stewart.

'He's still settling in,' Mum says. 'They do things different in the country.'

'Men do things different you mean. My Albert. Like pulling teeth, church is,' says Mrs Stewart.

'Dad says the good Lord knows where he is if He wants him,' says Emily.

'Still, good to know who shares a pew, isn't it, Jack? I'm not one of those prejudiced people. We've a family of Catholics right next door and we let their lad help around the yard. Not that I've ever been inside their house. Not that they've ever invited me. Probably wall to wall with statues of the Virgin

70

and no room for visitors at all.' She giggles. 'Emily's father has the hardware shop on Swan Street.'

'I'm forever down there getting new screws, paint for touching up, bits and bobs,' says Dad. 'What Albert doesn't know about varnish is nobody's business.'

'Not just varnish, Mr Husting. Nails too,' says Emily.

When they all sit I see there's an empty chair next to Emily. Mum looks at me. I stare at the chair, then I look at the front door. It's closed but the bolt isn't drawn. It's not far away. Half a dozen strides.

'Jack,' Mum says.

Parents raise and feed and clothe and educate us. A good education in my case. Ballarat Grammar, as befits the only nephew of a childless station owner. Geography and Latin and history. Sitting is not too much to ask. Come on, Jack. Knees, they're not made for decoration. They bend, given the right encouragement. There's cake, I see, with apricots and jam on top. Mum's got her hat on, the one she bought for my cousin Sarah's wedding. If they had given me a bit of notice I could have been prepared. Although, to be fair, if I'd known in advance I might be out the other side of Sunbury by now. I pull the chair out. I sit.

'There's an outdoor part where they stack the timber,' Mum says. 'A decent-sized yard. I've often wished our shop had a yard like that.'

I look up. First I've heard about that particular ambition.

'Half the work is outside, looking after the timber and whatnot,' says Mrs Stewart. 'My Albert really knows his timber.'

'Good storage, that's the trick,' says Emily. 'Warping, splitting. It's the damp that does it.'

She is sitting with her back straight, knees and feet together. Her gloved hands are folded in her lap and little dark circles of sweat are blooming between the fingers. Her legs are still, her waist is still, her ankles are still.

'Our Jack's very fond of timber,' says Mum. 'Well. Trees, at any rate. Knows one kind from another. Not just the normal ones, oaks and elms and so forth. The scrubby ones too. Gums and whatnot. And birds. Jack's fond of being outdoors. Aren't you, Jack? Fond of being outdoors? And of timber.'

'We have hoop pine and bunyah, mostly. From Queensland. For floors,' says Emily. 'And ash. Local, of course. Not New Zealand kauri. Can't get kauri anymore.'

'That so?' says Dad.

'Runned out,' says Emily.

My mother cuts the cake: large slabs for Dad and me, slender pieces for the ladies. Emily balances her plate on her lap in a delicate manner that's impossible to fault. She and her mother compliment the cake, the little forks, the napkins.

'Lovely,' she says. 'Crown Derby, is it?' Mum blushes parrot-pink, turns one plate over to show the maker's mark, the part that tells women what's what if they speak the language. I stare at the cake. The cake stares back, two apricot halves looking at me cross-eyed. I use my fork to break off a bit and force it down with a swig of tea.

'Emily only has sisters,' says Mum. 'Girls are a blessing for mothers but it must be hard on your father, dear.'

'Dad always says Mum shouldn't feel bad. He says he's sure she did as best she could.' She lays a glove on her mother's knee.

'A good husband,' Mrs Stewart says. 'And so generous with us girls.'

'For Christmas he bought us all stockings just like the Duchess of Kent's,' Emily says. 'Two-thread sheer. Colour of orchid bronze.'

'I'm sure you and our Jack would have a lot in common. Are you fond of the pictures? Our Jack loves going to the pictures, don't you Jack. And animals, I'll bet you're fond of animals. Our Jack was shoeing horses until recently on my brother's station, out west, near Darlington. Practically South Australia. Of course, that wasn't all he was doing. A very responsible position, wasn't it Jack, for so young a man? And,' she pauses until it seems that inspiration strikes. 'Very educational, shoeing horses. As far as nails.' She bestows a triumphant smile on Emily, who clearly has no idea what to do with this insight.

'You work as well,' Dad says. 'In the shop.'

'We all do. My sisters and me. Dad can't lift much, on account of his arm.'

'Shame.' Dad rubs both elbows. 'Best mark in the under-19s, Albert Stewart.'

'The Great War. That's where he lost it.' Emily shakes her head. 'In France, or somesuch.'

I have an image unbidden of the poor arm, wandering over foreign fields, trying to find its way home.

'Can't imagine him with two. That long ago,' says Mrs Stewart.

'He's a wonder, your father,' Mum says. 'And never any trouble with the drink.'

'He always says he'd rather be missing one arm than got gassed,' Emily says.

'Wicked, that gas,' says Mum. 'Credit to him that he never breathed it in.'

'He can do most everything except wash his hand and roll his shirt sleeve up and pin it and cut his nails. We girls take it in turns to do that, have since we were little. In the shop I work mostly inside. I'm in charge of washing machines.'

'Washing machines,' says Dad. 'That must be a good deal of responsibility for so young a lady. How old are you, Emily? Eighteen?'

'Nearly. Do you have a washing machine yourself, Mrs Husting?'

'I'm sure they're wonderful for a certain type of family,' Mum says, 'but I have a girl every Monday.'

'Our new vacuum washer, it has a copper plunger. The lightest silks and stockings can be washed in it. No boiling, no rubbing, no scrubbing.'

'Fancy,' says Mum.

There is more talk of washing machines but no further mention of stockings. There is talk about bicycles. Emily maintains they are the future of cheap transportation for working people. She believes it possible to cycle in a ladylike fashion and my mother's expression betrays her politely withheld disagreement. Emily also believes that horses will soon live only in zoos and every good family will have a car and, if her washing machines are any example, there will be so many labour-saving devices that women will have all day to practise drawing and needlework.

'Is that so, Emily?' says Mum. 'I'm sure I wouldn't know what to do with myself if my labour were to be saved.'

After an hour or so, Emily's mother says they must be getting back, and Mum says how nice it is that they've visited, and would she like to take some cake for her husband, bless him. They must come again.

I say goodbye and shake Emily's hand again. After they've gone, Dad says what a beaut girl, that she'll make some lad proud, and even with so many young men away a girl like Emily can have her pick of any fellow she likes. Then Mum says what a good little cook she is and what she can do with a bunny is nobody's business. And how her father is so clever, running the shop instead of becoming a lift driver or going on the susso like most one-armed men you see. It's a good job, though, lift driver, Dad says. A job for life. There'll always be a need for lift drivers; every new building in the city's taller than the last. Neither of Emily's sisters is married yet—they're plainer than she is and one has a trace of a moustache—and sure as eggs the first son-in-law will have his way with the shop. It's no McConchie's or Provan's, not yet. Modest. But it could be. My mother's eyes are shining.

———✦———

An hour later I find myself on the front step of the Westaways' in an ironed shirt and my good jacket, an old cane basket filled with lemons on my arm.

When the door opens I manage to keep my jaw from dropping. I am greeted by two boys standing together, peas in a pod, the same but different.

'Ma! There's someone here,' yells one of them. They're fine-boned with gangly limbs that don't quite fit right. One is thinner than the other. Their eyes are dark and deep-set, wide mouths and straight hair. I know Kip, he's the one who needs a haircut. The other one has a new-looking short back and sides.

'Mr Husting, hello,' says Kip. He shakes my hand. His nose is bent; someone's helped it to that shape. He's got a faded shiner and a cheeky grin, the kind of lad who'd have been a great ally in getting up to mischief when I was his age. It's a shame there's a good six years between us. I tell him it's good to meet him properly at last.

'You work right there and haven't met?' says the other.

Kip looks bashful. I raise my eyebrows and shrug. We nod at each other from time to time but truth be told, Kip's not allowed in the house. Mum says Catholic boys are odds on to have lice. And, for my part, the feel of Charlie and the smell of him and the warmth of his flank under my hand makes me want to saddle up and head west without even stopping to pack or say goodbye. Inside, I'm out of temptation's way.

'I'm out the back,' says Kip. 'Charlie sure is some horse.'

I suppose he probably is. Every boy thinks his first horse, his first love, is the only one for him. He'll never forget Charlie, not for the rest of his life.

The neater one shakes my hand, says *how do you do* and pronounces his name *Frarncis*. At boarding school he'd have his head beaten in for that kind of poncing. He's not the kind of boy whose friends call him Frank. I tell them to call me Jack.

Their mother appears behind them, Mrs Westaway, hands on her hips, hair loose and grey and hanging in her eyes. She might be the same age as my mother, younger maybe, but she has no padding. She is all sharp angles and tart features, her eyes chips of granite. I feel a surge of guilt that my father is alive. I tell them my mother sent me with lemons from the tree that's weighed down with fruit in our backyard.

'Your mother, indeed. Mrs Husting. Sent us over a basket of lemons.'

I don't trust myself to speak under her stare so I nod and she scowls and humphs, and then Connie Westaway comes up behind her. She's not wearing her apron now. Her dress is the colour of new wheat and her hair is almost black. Her nose has freckles carefully placed, as if with a pencil and a steady hand.

'How thoughtful.' She leans forward to take the basket. For an instant, her hand is next to mine. 'You must thank Mrs Husting for us. You can never have enough lemons.'

'I never saw that many lemons at your place,' says Kip.

'On the far side,' I say. 'Nearly pulled the tree over with the weight of them.'

He looks me square in the face. 'You'd think I'd of noticed a thing like that.'

'You'd be flat out working, I'd expect,' I say.

'They're lovely lemons,' says Connie. 'Aren't they boys?'

'They're heavy all right.' Kip lifts one, tosses and catches it. 'And they're good looking too. I've never seen anything quite so lemony.'

Francis shrugs. 'Things that grow in piles of manure are Kip's department, but they look just like normal lemons to me.'

'To me,' Kip says, 'they look just like the ones in the front of the shop on Swan Street that go for a shilling a bag.'

'How tall are you, Mr Husting? Six foot?' Connie says.

'Thereabouts.'

'I'm having some trouble with the washing line. It's come down, I'm afraid. Would you mind?'

We leave the boys—Kip with his forehead creased and puzzled—and Mrs Westaway, who is glaring. Connie leads me down the hall and through the kitchen where she tumbles the lemons into a bowl so I can take the basket back: a good idea; it'd be awkward if Mum misses it. In the backyard, it takes two shakes to fix the line. The far post's half down and needs knocking back in the ground, which I do with a half brick I see lying near the fence. It's on its last legs, though. It needs fixing before it collapses one day and a whole wash gets dragged in the dirt. I can bring a piece of timber from home and it'll be right as rain, I tell her.

She says thanks, looks at the clothes basket on the ground and tells me to hold out my arms straight. She takes off the shirts and towels one peg at a time, flicks them with a quick movement of her wrists so the edges line up crisp and straight, and lays them on my arms. It's as if her arms were dancing, just the way her feet were this morning. Take the peg off, then another, stretch the towel, flick and fold. Her skin is white and cream and pearl under the sun. There's a bracelet on her wrist. Rosy-gold, tiny clusters of grapes joined together. As she brings her hands up and down, the bracelet moves: first dangling at the top of her hand, then tight against the plump white flesh of her one arm. For a while, everything is quiet. Just the usual late-afternoon sounds; birds, kids playing, water running in a yard on the other side. A distant wireless.

'And where do you go to, then? At night?' She doesn't even look at me. She focuses on her task as though she's never in her life seen such fascinating towels before. 'After the lights go out next door.'

'Where do I go?'

She nods. 'At night. When everyone else is asleep in their beds.'

'Not everyone is asleep. You, for example. Or else you wouldn't notice that I go anywhere.'

She takes the pile from my arms and transfers it to the basket. She's folding a bed sheet now, holding it under her chin, stretching her arms wide. I take one end and we stand with the sheet stretched wide between us like a white river, then she walks towards me. Close, closer, she stretches out her arms and our fingertips touch as she joins my corners of the sheet to hers. 'Me and Mum share the front room. You try to be quiet but that's when people are the noisiest of all. And I'm not such a great sleeper myself.'

It strikes me that she'd understand. I've not said a word to Mum and Dad but they've never noticed and they've never asked. I met Connie Westaway, really met her, only ten minutes ago but I've seen her dancing with a broom around her backyard with no music. Something tells me she'd know what I meant if I told her about how the sky's different in the bush, about how the ceiling seems to press in at night. About how the only way I can sleep in that little room is if I let myself in at dawn so tired I can barely stand.

But instead I say, 'I'm sorry if I disturb you. I walk. Down by the river or through the city. Sometimes to the Botanic Gardens. That's all.'

'You're lucky. If I was a man, that's what I'd do all night long. Just walk and walk.' She doesn't ask why I walk. She seems to know already.

'The city's not the same in the dark.'

She nods. 'Why would it be? Nighttime's not just daytime with the sun gone. It's different entirely. After Ma and the boys are asleep it's like I'm the only one here alive and the whole world belongs to me.'

'You should see the dark in the bush. You can just about touch the dark. You can feel it on your fingertips.'

'Why did you come back, then? To the wilds of Richmond?'

I would tell her if I knew. Instead I stand here in the Westaways' backyard holding sheets, tongue-tied. Connie Westaway has an easy way of talking. As if we're not really strangers, as if she's known me all her life. She has a new job, at the *Argus*. Her boss is very kind. She is an assistant to the photographers. She files their photos, types up labels, keeps track of their jobs, cares for their cameras. Sometimes she goes out with them, sometimes they let her hold the camera and even take a picture, although she is still learning. It seems too much for her some days, she says, on her feet morning till night then cooking for the boys and cleaning when she gets home. Yet even this is not enough to make her want to sleep. And she loves the photographs.

'Your memory fades,' she says. 'But not the pictures. They're just like real life, except flat and crisp. That's what I like about them. They last forever. One day I'm going to be a photographer myself.'

I hear a muffled snort from the side of the house and two shiny faces appear.

'The Shadow knows!' yells Kip, as he leaps around the corner.

I never listen to the wireless but even I know The Shadow is really Lamont Cranston, an American crime-busting hero, worshipped by boys the world over.

Francis is behind Kip. 'The Shadow. Honestly, Kip. You're such a baby.' He rolls his eyes to include us all in his sweeping disdain. 'A girl photographer.' He raises his arms and pulls on the clothes line, which explains its condition. 'That's stupid.'

'It's not that different from being an artist,' Connie says. 'It's about imagining a picture and making it real. You have to think ahead to what the photograph will look like when everyone can see it. The kind of story it'll tell. Look, Kip. See that wall there? See where the light hits it?' She holds the boy by his shoulders and turns him so he's facing the side of the house, then points to the edge of sunlight as it shines on the boards. 'It looks closer, doesn't it? But it isn't. It's the light that makes it seem that way.' She makes a rectangle out of her thumbs and index fingers and peers through them. Kip stands in front of her and does the same.

'The light decides where you look first,' she says.

Kip nods. 'The light's boss and your eyes just do as they're told.'

'It's not a respectable job, a photographer.' Francis leans against the back of the house. 'It's dicey. Like working at Rosella when the fruit comes in. A good job's a steady job. At a desk, in the government.'

'Connie had something in the paper just last week, didn't you, Connie?' Kips says. 'Tell Jack about the umbrella. Connie makes suggestions sometimes.'

She smiles, and for the first time it strikes me that in different company she might be shy. 'For the fashion pages, mostly.'

'Last Monday she came up with the idea that one of the models oughta be holding an umbrella over one shoulder, and sure enough that's the one that went in the paper,' he says.

'Lucky,' she says.

'I'd want to take pictures of fires and car accidents,' says Francis. 'Fashion. Who cares about that?'

'You will, soon enough,' I say. 'Fashion's all about pretty girls.'

'She only got the job because of Dad anyway. He was a typesetter. That's why Mr Ward took her on. Ma says that's why he's spoiling her rotten. Driving her home and giving her chocolates and buying her dinner when they work late. Because of Dad.'

'Is it true you know how to shoe a horse?' says Kip.

There's no more talk of photography, or of Mr Ward. I tell Kip about Jasper, who can find his own way home using the stars, who never needs tethering, who can carry two men for hours without failing but, it seems, is inferior to Charlie in every way. The sun is setting. I hadn't realised how much time has passed. I say my goodbyes and the three of them walk me down to the side gate.

'Thanks again for the lemons,' Connie says.

Kip shakes his head. 'A whole shilling. There's one born every minute.'

When I get home, I ask Mum about the Westaways. How they've been since Tom Westaway passed. She does not approve of Connie's new job.

'She seemed such a nice girl,' Mum says, over tea. She asks if I'd like more mash and when I say no, she piles another dollop on. 'Everyone in the street worried when they lost the boarder. She was a decent woman, never married, never had any visitors. Always had time for a hello, more than you can say for that Jean Westaway. Having a boarder is a respectable way for a Catholic family to improve themselves. Then we heard Connie'd got a job. First we all thought it'd be good for her, good for the whole family. She looks a picture in her new suit and stockers, her hair set properly instead of that ponytail. Pretty girl, colouring's not too Irish. Maybe a bit broad across the face.'

'Not everyone can have features as refined as yours, love,' says Dad. He doesn't catch my eye.

Mum picks up Dad's plate and scrapes the beans on to mine. 'They repeat on your father.'

I scoop up the beans, soft and grey, on the side of my fork.

'Viking cheekbones in our family, my pa used to say,' says Mum. 'Lucky for Jack he takes after my people. Look at that jawline. Doesn't Emily have nice cheekbones? You can always tell breeding by the cheekbones.'

The trouble with Connie Westaway's job, as I hear when I express interest, is not only that a newspaper is not a respectable place to work, but that Connie does not keep decent hours. She is often home late, dropped off by her boss, who has a car. The dapper Mr Ward, a widower with two small boys, should take more care. He should have an eye to propriety with a young girl in his employ. In fact, the news is this: Mrs Westaway confided in Joyce Macree in Tanner Street who told Mrs Arnold the draper's wife who told Mum in the strictest confidence that Mrs Westaway has hopes for Mr Ward. She's almost sure there'll be an engagement soon, in spite of the age gap. Then Connie won't be able to work.

And there's no denying the difference it would make to that family. Mrs Arnold says Ward's been in for tea and agrees that Francis is a serious boy and must go to the university and that takes money, even with a scholarship. The boys and their mother might even go live with them in his big house in Hawthorn. Although even then, Mum says, Kip will never make anything of himself, ('that's plain'), and if we have to send boys to fight overseas—here she gives me a nervous glance—'it's layabout boys with no responsibilities, the Kip Westaways of the world, who ought to be going'.

For afters my mother serves the remains of the apricot cake and tells me that people are happier if they stay where they belong and don't try to become something they're not. As indisputable evidence she tells me a story of the O'Riordan girl from Highett Street who Sid Lindsay got involved with and how badly that turned out for all concerned. If she was advising Connie Westaway, Mum would be telling her *don't forget your place*. But if Connie's set her cap at Ward, then it's high time there was an engagement. Girls can't be too careful. Far be it from Mum to suggest the girl's done anything wrong, despite the absence of a father's influence; sometimes when the man's a drinker a family's better off without him. And the mother. Mum purses her lips in that particular shape that means *common*. Still, there's nothing to say that Connie's let herself down. 'It's a shame,' my mother concludes, 'that the world is so full of gossips.'

When I go up to my room after dinner, there're curtains on the window. New, tight on the rail, difficult to pull open. Red and white checks.

———————

That night, instead of walking down to the Cremorne stretch of the river, I lean on the fence across the street from the Westaways'. The light in Connie's window is still on. Now and then I can see a shape moving behind the curtain. If she opened her window she'd see me standing here. She's reading or maybe sewing. Thinking about her photographs, about her future married to her newspaperman and raising his boys, being her family's saviour. She is breathing the same air as me, on the same street.

It's good that Connie has found someone to look after her, someone with money in the bank and a good job and a house. Someone who might take her dancing, someone who plans to live in this city for good and won't take her away from her family. Mum says they've lived next door since I was a toddler. Just a fence away. I think and I think, but I can't remember one story, not one detail. What a fool I've been.

After a while I move off from just staring at her room because it feels as if there's something not quite right about that, something a man should be ashamed of. I keep walking until I reach the river. By moonlight it looks like beaten pewter, lumpy with rubbish. I think of Emily's father and his shop. *He can do almost everything*, she said, but I can't imagine him riding a horse, or fencing or shearing. I might be a coward but I'd rather be lost along with the arm than safe without it, regardless of the guaranteed employment as a lift operator. One day a soldier of the empire facing the Hun for King and country; the next a grown man sitting on a stool in a tiny box ferrying men with soft hands up and down. I think of Emily and her sisters as little girls, their tiny palms and fingers smoothing soap and water over that big calloused hand. His humility, their tenderness. Drying the hand with a towel, patting it as if he were a doll. But even this image stirs no feeling in me.

Tonight, no matter where I walk or what I see, I am still in the Westaways' yard watching Connie fold towels with her quick hands. I think about living next door when the news of her engagement does the rounds. Looking down from my little window as she goes off to the church. Her mother shining with pride; Connie ready to take her husband's hand and begin her big adventure. I wonder how long it'll take to get Mum and Dad sorted. I wonder what time the drill hall opens.

That first night when I got home—not home, I can't say home—that first night when I got to my parents' house, I still had the rattle of the train in my body. I swayed down the hall and had to convince Mum I'd not stopped at the pub. That first night—before I'd twigged to tiptoe down the hall in my stockinged feet, boots in my hand, and let myself out the front door ten minutes after their lights went out—that night, I didn't know how I'd get to sleep. I tried to keep the old man up with me. We sat in the front room and I told him stories about every shearer and every sheep and about Jasper till his eyes were hanging out on stalks. *Can't get a word out of him during the day*, he said, shaking his head. *Come bed time, can't shut him up.* I said I'd toss him: heads, ten more minutes; tails, off to bed now.

The poor bugger. He's an early riser, always was. He couldn't stand it any longer. *I'll have to call it a day, son*, he said, as I sent my coin spinning. *No need to squeeze it all into one night.* He grabbed it right out of the air. Plucked it like a lemon when it paused at the top of its flight and put it in his pocket. Pity. It wasn't just any old coin. It won me my new saddle in a two-up school last winter, back on the station. That was my lucky shilling.

CHAPTER FOUR

Charlotte

THERE IT IS again, that slight heaviness in my abdomen that I felt as I rolled on my side during the night. Not a twinge, exactly. More a weight. A disturbance in the flesh. I feel it as I stretch my arms above my head at the beginning of *surya namaskar* and again in *vriksana*. The sole of my foot presses against the mat and the toes are spread, firm but not clenching. I breathe and feel my muscles respond, loosen. The first class of the day brings the energy of the sun and these familiar poses balance and awaken and empower. The air is still bracing; these old heaters take some time. The class is lined up before me, concentrating. They have not noticed anything amiss. They are following my movements, my instructions for each pose, but I do not feel balanced.

There is something here that is not right.

'Draw the flesh of the right inner thigh outward,' I say. 'Engage the thigh muscle. Engage the knee. Pull the skin on the inside of the left leg towards the back of the room.'

Some in the class are fluid and some are not. My heart goes out to the stiff ones, the way they try week after week, struggling with something that does not come easily. It gives me hope. It reminds me of the resilience and determination of life.

'Soften the face, soften the breath.'

When I say this, they all concentrate on being soft. They see no contradiction in this. They do not understand the courage that is required simply to surrender. It makes me smile.

I sometimes take the evening class but this early one, before the sun is up, is the busiest of the whole day. It's mat flush against mat—black for the boys, purple for the girls—all of them office workers or executives in their shorts and leotards. The men have this intense focus like they're negotiating a corporate takeover in the middle of downward dog; the women's hair is pulled back tight and they wear lipstick and mascara and earrings. Their suits hang in the change rooms: supermen and wonderwomen. They leave sharpened, ready for their day to begin. I cherish a hope that this morning peace they hold in their hearts will make them kinder accountants and bankers, more understanding real estate agents. I told Stanzi this once.

She shook her head. 'No chance. Hitler did a mean downward dog and he didn't start to mellow till he got to Stalingrad.'

I'm almost positive Hitler didn't practise yoga, but there's no use correcting Stanzi when she thinks she's being funny.

When I was a teenager and first learning yoga, my teacher always started the class with a chant. We beginners sat on blankets or bolsters in our best attempt at legs crossed and said the words along with her, clear and loud, earnest like a spell. Only it wasn't a spell. It was Sanskrit, and none of us knew what it meant. Sometimes in those beginning classes, I imagined all those serious people struggling to perfect their yoga and chanting: *two beef patties special sauce lettuce cheese pickles onions on a sesame seed bun* in Sanskrit. Chanting still makes me want to smile, but I don't laugh out loud in class anymore.

After the class, my muscles sit better on my bones and my head balances high of its own accord but that foreign feeling in my abdomen remains. I wrap myself up in layers and as I walk up the hill in the dawn light, I see a cloud of seagulls swoop along the beach and settle in the carpark. It's heartening. Even though birds are utterly free, they choose to flock. They prefer to be with their kind. There's a sense of connection, I guess. An invisible thread. The birds rise again as one, soar over the road and start to squabble over a box of chips spilt in the gutter. I notice a gull standing on one leg; her other is hooked under her, toes hanging loose and wobbling as she balances. She hops towards a chip and loses it to a more agile friend. I wonder how a bird can survive such an injury, and whether she had it from birth. Then I see it: the glisten of a filament. She has fishing line wrapped tight around her claw. It is close to severed.

And there is nothing I can do. If I approach she will fly away, if I grab the dangling line I will make the injury worse. We humans fuck everything up, everything. I look at the seagull and it's all I can do not to cry so I keep walking. The birds scatter, even the damaged one. The person responsible for that fishing line: karma better not forget about them. Stanzi would tell me to get a grip. I remember as a child spending ages every morning choosing which shoes I would wear and then worrying all day about the poor ones left behind in the cupboard, about how dejected they must feel having been passed over. Forsaken. I tried explaining it to Stanzi but she thought I was joking.

The tram is on time and as we go by, Luna Park smiles at me and I feel better. I smile back. Wherever you are, whatever you're doing, you can usually find something to make you smile. You just have to look for a sign.

———————+———————

At work, the roller door is already up. Craig is on time even though Sandra is in Daylesford for the weekend. He looks like he's slept. His hair is smoothed down and he's even shaved, a bit. He looks good with a little growth. Whiskers help him keep a sense of mystery about the line of his jaw. He is frowning like a little boy pretending to be grown up. The shop key hangs around his neck attached to a lanyard so everyone can see he's the trusted one. It's very cute. He's checking the change in the till and has the order books spread across the counter.

'We're out of garlic tablets.' He doesn't look up.

'How? We got a delivery last week.'

I don't know who sells so much garlic. Perhaps it's Kylie. I always tell her: garlic in a tablet is great to kickstart the immune system but for chronic conditions, she should focus on the diet. Wheat and dairy, out. Preservatives, out.

I put my coat and gloves and scarf in the storeroom. When I get back, he's stacking the special bread orders on the bottom shelf. He never bends his knees when he leans over. It's shocking for his back. Craig looks calm, but I can tell he's not. He's got them out of alphabetical order.

'Where were you?' He still hasn't looked at me.

'I fancied a quiet night. I meditated for a while then I read. That's all.'

'You might have said you weren't coming. I left a ticket for you on the door.'

He practically throws the yeast-free up on the top shelf. One packet zooms across the top and flops to the floor. Craig stomps back to the counter. There is no *ticket for you on the door*. There are no tickets of any kind. There is no cover charge: the band gets ten dollars, a counter dinner and three beers each. Craig's mouth is like a child's drawing of a sad person.

'I'm sorry.' I pick up the bread, dust it off and put it back on the shelf.

'It's cool. Don't come if you don't want to.'

He looks at me then and I see his eyes. His eyes are soft and brown with long lashes, wet, deep Bambi eyes. It's impossible to look into them without falling. Almost as soon as I met him I started thinking about how those eyelashes would feel brushing my skin, how it would feel to kiss those eyes closed.

'Sorry.'

'I mean, I'd hate to put you out or anything.'

Take a deep breath, Craig, I think. I send him messages of peace and tranquility. *Relax, Craig. Imagine the sun's light pouring through the top of your head and coming out your chakras in different colours. Think sky-blue thoughts.*

He doesn't relax. He trudges to the fridge, opens it, stares inside, then closes it again. Then he tramps back to the counter. 'Last night was important to me, Charlotte. You know that. We've been practising our new material.'

He looks so distressed. If he keeps this up, he'll get a headache. He needs to sit down. If he sat down, I could rub his shoulders. He likes that. I reach into the bottom cupboard and find the oil burner, then look through the half-opened bottles to find something calming. Maybe Roman Chamomile and Clary Sage? 'How did it go? The new material?'

'Really well. Good. Fine. Jesus, Charlotte, you might have come.'

I set the oil burner next to the cash register. Matches. Where are the matches? 'You don't need me there every night, surely. I bet the crowd loved you. I bet you were a smash.'

'Jon and Jamie's girlfriends come. They sit at the bar and get the clapping started. It's called support.'

'I was tired.' I light the burner. Soon he'll start to feel better.

'That clapping. It's bloody exhausting, isn't it?' He claps, slowly, in case I have an incomplete grasp of the concept.

94

'I didn't realise they took attendance. It's just a bar. You play almost every week.'

'Fine.' He turns back to counting the change. 'Be like that.'

I pout and reach up to kiss him. 'Poor baby. Turn that frown upside down.'

'Fuck off.'

'How about a coffee? I'll open a fresh soy milk and you can tell me all about last night. What did you play first?'

He ignores me. I shrug. Scorpios. There's nothing you can do. You can't control the whole world.

The sign comes just after my lunch break. Craig needs some space so I make a ginger tea and spend most of the morning in the store room. There are deliveries to be unpacked, invoices to tick off, dates to check. Soon one of the reps will visit and try to sell us the wrong thing: a new pill for younger skin or weight loss, a cream that says 'fills wrinkles from the inside' in gold swirly letters on the label. A few times I hear Craig's voice speaking to a customer and the juicer starts up. I think about wrapping my arms around him and telling him the real reason I didn't go out last night, even though I'm not certain, even though I'm probably wrong.

At eleven, he pokes his head around the door. 'Customer for you,' he says. He can see I'm busy. He's good with the customers. He could do this himself.

But when I come out, I understand. Craig listens to the old ladies talk about the bulbous joints and thready memory, the middle-aged women talk about menopause in forensic detail, even the blushing girls describe their period paid. He has what Sandra calls 'strong feminine energy'. Sometimes the girls from the convent school drop by for a smoothie, and to giggle and give him sideways glances. He knows what he's doing, too: he dropped out of naturopathy with only one semester to go. He's practically a professional. There's only one kind of customer he's not so good with.

In the middle of the centre aisle is a young woman with a stroller, and in the stroller is a sleeping blonde girl, two or three maybe, soft curls on her face under a beanie, dressed in a pre-feminist pink coat with a Disney princess on her stockings. Her cheeks are flushed and there's a crust of snot around her nostrils. It only takes a second to see the white line across the bridge of her nose.

The woman smiles. 'She seems to get colds all the time.' She brushes the girl's damp fringe. 'I was thinking she needs something to build her up. Boost her resistance.'

It's a typical story, this time of year. It's what people come in for. All around us are bottles, pills and potions, herbs and extracts. It's not that I disapprove. There's something soothing about them. They contain all the hopes of the human spirit, all the refusal to quit, to keep believing people can feel better. The herbs are evidence of an understanding of our place in the universe. The minerals and vitamins are a return to the earth, an acknowledgement of the delicate balance in our bodies, the need for things that come from the soil or the sun. The woman in front of me is well dressed with sparkly stones on her fingers. The stroller is the expensive European variety. I could probably sell her anything. I kneel next to the girl and she wakes with an almighty sneeze that I only just manage to dodge.

'Bless you,' I say.

Waking to find a stranger peering at you is disconcerting, yet the girl doesn't make a sound. Her eyes are blue like mine and big as the sea. She purses her bud lips and rubs her nose. A silvery trail remains on the back of her tiny hand.

The woman pretends not to notice the snot. 'The lady said "bless you". What do we say, Charlotte?'

The girl blinks.

'We say "thank you".'

The woman is towering over the child, who says nothing. Seconds tick by. The mother becomes embarrassed. She is torn between adopting a sterner voice to show that she is not to be trifled with, or letting it slide. Either way she risks being seen as a poor mother. An ego standoff. The silence is pressing but the girl doesn't notice. Willful disobedience always makes me smile.

'Charlotte? That's a pretty name.' I force my hand to stay where it is and not touch her. Her hair would feel as soft as a kitten. 'It's my name too.'

'Isn't that funny? I named her after Charlotte Brontë.'

'Really? Which of her books do you like best?'

'Oh.' The woman pauses and glides her tongue along the front of her teeth. 'I like them all.'

She kneels now and fusses with the girl's coat and beanie, smoothing the ruffles and running her fingers under the stroller straps that hold her in place. The girl wriggles as though she'd forgotten she was restrained until her mother reminded her.

I didn't set out to trick that poor woman. I like to see what people are really like. She couldn't name *Jane Eyre*. Even if she knew it once, even if she read it while she was pregnant, she has since lost confidence in the things she used to know and the person she once was. Perhaps she is almost certain the book is *Jane Eyre*, but what if she is wrong? Just in case the right answer is *Wuthering Heights*, she will say nothing. She is the kind of woman who cannot risk even a shop assistant, who is unlikely to have read Brontë and does not know her and whom she will never meet again, catching her out in a mistake. Wrapped up in *I like them all* is every bit of her vulnerability. I want more than anything to live in the kind of world where I could give her a hug.

'I was named after my father's best friend when he was a boy,' I say instead. 'Except he wasn't a Charlotte. He was a Charlie.'

'What do you think about that, Charlotte? The lady was named after a boy!' Charlotte is nonplussed. 'Your father's friend must have been proud.'

'They lost touch well before I was born. Charlie moved to the country or something. Dad says he still thinks about him after all these years.'

'Huh. So do you think she needs a tonic?'

'What she needs is less dairy and wheat. She has an intolerance.'

We have a long discussion about the antigens in grains, and pesticides, and the lack of nutrients in conventionally grown vegetables. She says, *it's so hard, raising children today.* I show her ancient grain cereals without cane sugar and preservatives. She says, *Charlotte's such a fussy eater. No vegetables at all. And for lunch, cheese sticks. That's it.* I didn't know that cheese came in a stick, but I doubt that Charlotte drives to Coles and buys them herself. I show her sheep's yoghurt, popcorn for snacks, corn chips made from organic corn. *We didn't have food intolerances when I was a girl.* I tell her the line across her daughter's nose is the result of continual itchiness: the child sniffs and pushes the end of her nose up with the back of her hand so often it leaves a white mark because the sun can't reach it. *All she'll eat for dinner is sausage and chips. And Kentucky Fried. I'm just glad she's eating something.* The white band on the girl's nose is distinct and distinctive. Like so many things that shape us, it's the smallest actions that add up to leave the deepest marks.

The woman takes one of the cereals I hand her and runs her fingers down the ingredient list. 'Hmmm,' she says. 'Is there a toy in the box?'

<hr />

'If Sandra was here, you'd be shot,' Craig says, when the woman and her daughter leave. 'A box of cereal. You spent all that time with her and that's it.'

'That's all she needed.'

'Ascorbic acid, at the very least. Homoeopathics. Just as well you're not on commission. You'd be earning less than you do now, if that's humanly possible.' He walks to the cereal aisle and moves all the boxes forward one spot to replace the one the woman bought. 'She won't use it, you know. She just bought the cheapest one because she didn't know how to get out of it.'

'She's worried about her little girl. She'll use it. She'll be back for more in a couple of weeks and she'll get the corn chips too. You'll see.'

He leans against the fridge with his arms folded. 'She's probably in Coles buying a box of something with extra dairy, wheat, sugar and artificial everything. She was being polite. They'll both have doughnuts and a soft drink for lunch in the food court. Your box'll go in the bin as soon as they get home.'

'It won't. Every mother wants what's best for her child.'

'You should have sold her a bottle of tablets. People like that only trust tablets.'

'"People like that"? Who are "people like that"?'

He shakes his head. 'If you can't tell the bourgeois when you see them, there's no hope for you.'

Craig's parents live in Brighton. His friends from school sometimes come to hear him play. They drink Crown Lager and by the end of the night they can't stand up. Last week, one lurched out the front door and vomited on the footpath in the middle of the final set. Craig's school tie still hangs in his wardrobe. If Craig's the expert on picking the bourgeois, he's right. There's no hope for me.

'It's not easy, raising children. It's an enormous commitment. The most important job in the world.'

He rolls his eyes. 'It's not curing smallpox. It means you've fucked someone.'

'Don't you think she was a beautiful little girl?' I keep my voice casual. 'Gorgeous, wasn't she?'

'I guess.'

'What colour was your hair, when you were little?'

'I have no idea. I was small at the time.'

'Don't you want children some day?' I turn my back and move some bottles around on the shelf.

'Get real. The self-centred middle class, desperate to clone themselves to feed their ego. The mess the planet's in now. You'd have to be a moron.'

Craig is wrong. It's almost spring, the traditional time for rebirth. We are near the dawning of a new age, only one decade away from a pristine millennium. Last November, I stood in front of an electrical goods store in Smith Street and watched televisions showing huge crowds standing on the Berlin Wall. Just this February I sobbed at the pictures of Nelson Mandela leaving prison, hand in hand with Winnie. After all these centuries of causing our own pain, we are finally getting it. The planet is righting itself. I can feel it.

I can't wait any longer. It has to be done. I tell Craig I'm not feeling well and leave him to mind the shop. He can ring Kylie and see if she's available at short notice. She always is, when he's the one to ring. He'll sulk for a while but he'll be over it tomorrow.

———◆———

At home, Daisy and Jimbo are sitting out the back wrapped in blankets, sharing a spliff. They ask me to join them but instead I go to my room where the traffic noise is hushed. I light a candle and some incense. I take off my clothes and stand in front of the mirror and look at myself, at the miracle of my body. The skin is stippled with cold. It is strong and healthy and does what I tell it. I am blessed. The female body is the source of all life. It is the body of the living Goddess. We should have statues of it on every street corner, of women of all shapes and sizes, instead of dead explorers and hanging judges.

I open my underwear drawer. At the bottom next to my vibrator is a small inlaid jewellery box. I should wear these things more often but somehow I feel foolish, adorning myself in front of the mirror. I've never understood the concept of jewellery; how draping yourself with pretty things like a Christmas tree is supposed to make you look prettier. It makes you look plainer. Regardless of how smooth and even your skin is, it will always look dull next to a precious metal or a gem.

There is a sparkly brooch from an op shop, a bracelet of amber beads. Nestled in the middle is my mother's pendant, the one she gave me for my eighteenth. An amethyst pendant on a gold chain. At first, she didn't want to part with it. A classic problem: one pendant, two daughters. Stanzi said she didn't mind. She said she'd rather have cash, then used the money for the deposit on her car.

I hold the pendant between my hands, I hold it close to my heart, I hold it above the incense burning on my dresser. I close my eyes and say a few words to the universe. I am its child. I know the universe is listening.

I lie on the floor naked. The boards are cold and rough on

my spine and there's something down here that smells funny. I hold my mother's pendant tight in my fist above my belly. I centre myself for a few minutes then I drop the pendant down on the length of its chain, hold it directly over my stomach. Hold my breath, still my hand. Soon the pendant will move of its own accord. I wait, and after a few moments it begins to circle, slowly, anti-clockwise. I'm pregnant.

'A rotating pendant,' Stanzi says. 'Wow. Stop right there. Let me call the *British Medical Journal*.'

It's my own fault. When the pendant started circling, I was overwhelmed. I couldn't centre myself. There was only one place I could go: my sister's. I threw on my clothes and cycled straight here and paced back and forth in front of her building until she drove up. I couldn't wait. I blurted it out in the stairwell. We are now sitting at her dining table with the heater on full whack. She's not even wearing a jumper. In front of us are a bottle of white wine from her fridge and two glasses. Wine glasses. With stems. They match. They are not Vegemite jars with remnants of the label showing finger-nail scrapes. My glass is nearly full, hers nearly empty. I don't drink wine, she knows that. We have very different lives. We do not even look the same anymore, although I know under that flesh is a woman the same as me. Right now, she doesn't seem impressed.

'I can see the story now. *Hospitals around the world put their multi-million dollar diagnostic equipment out on the footpath for hard waste pickup and nip over to Tiffany's, thanks to medical breakthrough by naked shop assistant slash part-time yoga instructor dangling her mother's pendant over her beaver.'*

'It was my uterus. And it wasn't really Mum's pendant. I mean, it was, but I was using it as a pendulum. I'd cleared it already. A smoking ceremony.'

'Oh. A smoking ceremony. That's different.'

'Plus, I'm late. Two weeks. I'm never late. Plus, I've gone off coffee. That's conclusive.'

'Did you pee on the pendant and watch it make little blue lines? Because that's how it's done, Charlotte.'

'I'll do a test if you want. I have nothing against technology. But I know my body.'

'Right. Is that why I am sitting here talking to someone who allegedly knows her body about her unplanned pregnancy? Body, one. Charlotte, nil.'

'This sarcasm is only hurting you. It's your cynicism that prevents you being happy.'

'Actually it's my unhappiness that prevents me being happy, but let's not talk about me. Just tell me it isn't that complete moron Craig. Tell me it's someone else. A guy from that halfway house for the malodorous unkempt you live in. It's him, isn't it? Craig.' She downs her wine then reaches for mine and takes a swig, then rests her arms on the table and buries her head. Her voice is half-muffled by her soft white arms. 'Who would have thought his sperms had the energy to make it up there?'

'He's young. He's a wonderful bass player. Very caring with the customers. He's got a lot of potential.'

'Every half inch they'd be asking *are we there yet?*' She lifts her head and grimaces. 'They'd get to the cervix and stop for a round of applause and a podium ceremony. Besides, he's not young. He's twenty-four, like us.'

'Women mature faster than men.'

'What if it takes after him. Oh. My. God. A hippy groovy baby with Craig's loser gene. This is a complete disaster.'

She doesn't mean to be hurtful. She is worried for me, that's all. It's reassuring. It shows how much she cares, and besides, if she really thought I was in terrible trouble, she would be gentler. Her manner is a measure of the trust she places in me. It tells me I am strong. It tells me that she knows everything will be all right.

When I don't reply, she hoists herself to her feet. I can see from her face that it hurts. That's all the meat and grains she eats causing acid production in her joints. Not to mention sugar. Eating sugar is like pouring ground glass in your cartilage. I can't imagine what shape her intestinal flora must be in. Poor Stanzi. I could write her out a menu plan if only she'd do what she was told.

'Stay. Here. Do not go anywhere. Watch some TV. Oh, that's right. It's an evil tool of our corporate overlords designed to hypnotise us into buying useless trinkets to mask our deep-seated satisfaction with our meaningless lives caused by being out of touch with our spirituality and the energy of the planet. Better not watch TV then. I'm going down to the pharmacy for an actual pregnancy test that's had double-blind clinical trials, something manufactured by the ill-treated wage-slaves of a corrupt conglomerate. Something that's been tested on rats.'

When she's gone, I sit on her puffy couch but it's leather so I move to a cushion on the floor and try to meditate but I can't concentrate on my mantra. There is something growing inside me, a mass of cells splitting and re-splitting every second.

It'd be different if Stanzi was pregnant. Stanzi's going places. She has a degree. That dingy little office next to the dentist, that's temporary. She's only working as a counsellor until she saves up enough to do her PhD. She's going to be a psychoanalyst, the philosophical, Freudian type, unpicking people's fears from the inside. She has a proper career plan.

I have two casual jobs, no qualifications, no money. She rents a one-bedroom flat of her own. I live in a share house where you're considered anal retentive if you scrape the mould off last week's lentil soup before you eat it. She is back in twenty minutes and it seems like three. She hands me a packet.

'Here. Follow the directions. Can you manage that?'

When I shut the toilet door behind me, I nearly pass out. This is worse than that time I went to Chadstone. There are smells coming from everywhere and for a moment I can't breathe. The bowl has one smell—maybe bleach—the air itself has another courtesy of the aerosol can on the shelf. Even the toilet paper smells bizarrely of synthetic flowers. There are thousands of microscopic aromatics invading my lungs simultaneously. She'll get cancer if she keeps this up.

'Hey,' I yell, through the closed door. 'Why is the water in your toilet bowl blue?'

'Because orange stripes are so last year,' she yells back.

I balance the stick on my leg and almost drop the

instructions in the blue bowl. 'How do I tell when it's midstream? How can I possibly know in advance how long I'll pee for?'

'For God's sake. Make a guess,' she yells. 'Did you fail half-arsed at hippy school?'

Eventually I come out with the stick in my hand.

'Let me see, let me see.' She takes it from me, holds it gingerly between her thumb and forefinger. 'Well. The judges give round one to the pendant.'

'I want to see Mum.' I don't know why. All at once I feel this overwhelming need to be held by her.

'Are you sure? Charlotte, listen. I'm being serious now. You don't have to talk about this right away. You can think about it for a while. It can just be between us. You can tell them later.'

'I want to see Mum.'

'They're not home. She told me on the phone yesterday: they're at Uncle Frank's for dinner. It'll have to wait.'

'No. I need to see her now.'

She walks to the hall table and picks up her keys. 'Uncle Frank's it is then.' Then she stops. 'Oh my God.' She takes a few steps and drops into a chair, face in her hands. 'Dad.'

———✦———

Our father is the most loving man I know. He knows the bitter-sweet of twin-dom; when we were little, he knew when to encourage our independence and when to respect our bonds. He taught us to take life with a light heart and he did this in the most unexpected way. He impressed on us that we would die. That one day would be our last. He told us death is always around the corner.

This sounds bonkers, I know. Stanzi shakes her head at the memory of it. *What a way to speak to kids*, she says. If a parent did that today, someone would call community services.

But I knew what he meant. He meant there was no excuse not to take every day with two hands and wring the juice out of it. He wouldn't tolerate self-pity from us, or embarrassment, or fear. *Ring that boy*, or *try out for the musical*, or *ignore that pustulating zit on your chin. Don't take yourself so damn seriously. Soon you'll be six feet under and who'll care about it then? Nobody.*

In my whole life, I've only seen him angry once: the time he found Mark Moretti in my room after the year twelve formal and chased him out of the house with a golf club. I wanted to die.

It wasn't having Mark in my room that made Dad angry. When he first found us together, he actually grinned a little. He said *Oops* and went to close the door. Then he turned back and asked if we had a condom. I hated even hearing my father use that word. I looked at Mark. Mark looked at me. We were flushed and sweaty from the dancing and spiked punch. My dress was mauve taffeta, unzipped at the back.

I'd seen my father every day of my life but never like that. It wasn't wild and uncontrolled, not fury. He was yelling but his face was ice. 'Get the fuck out of my house,' he said to Mark, and he went downstairs to get a golf club from his study and I've still never seen anyone move as quickly as Mark that day, bolting out the door in his socks. As for me, I was irresponsible. I was thoughtless and stupid and a disgrace. For three days, I couldn't look at Dad.

And now I'm a grown woman, no longer living under their roof, responsible for my own body and my own fertility. I want to see my mother, but that means seeing Dad too. And something tells me nothing's changed.

———

We sit in Stanzi's car out the front of Uncle Frank's house in Rowena Parade. The engine is on, for the heater. Neither of us has moved. We haven't even taken off our seat belts.

Sometimes I think my parents come here so Dad can visit the house rather than Uncle Frank. This is where they grew up. Rowena Parade runs across the slope of the hill. It's wide for a Richmond street: cars park on both sides. It's halfway up the hill. Uncle Frank's house is a tiny weatherboard cottage with a lane at the side and at the back. It sits under the shadow of a double-storey house, a former shop-front across the side lane, and it's joined to a row of terraces on the other side. It's hard to imagine Dad and Uncle Frank as boys here. Two bedrooms, one bathroom attached at the back. Mum says Uncle Frank only had the toilet brought inside ten years ago. Too small even for three people but there were five at one stage. Their sister and my grandfather both died within a few years of each other when Dad and Uncle Frank were teenagers. Then, Richmond was famed for its slums: grown men killed from falling out of trams, healthy twenty-year-old girls dying from the flu. Richmond was another planet.

This house couldn't be more different from Mum and Dad's sprawling Federation triple-fronter in Malvern. There they've left our rooms untouched, down to the Duran Duran (me) and Buzzcocks (Stanzi) posters on the wall. The garden is azaleas and magnolias interspersed with irises and jonquils and lilies in the spring. My father planted those bulbs back when Mum was pregnant with Stanzi and me and twenty-five years later they still bloom. Love letters sent through time, from a sweetheart long ago. At Rowena Parade, there's hardly any garden. Uncle Frank has cemented over everything.

'You don't have to have it, you know.'

'I know.'

'They'll have finished dinner by now. Hospital hours. They haven't seen us. We can just drive away and they'd be none the wiser.'

'Yep.'

'We can go to that styrofoam place on Bridge Road. My treat.'

By this she means my favourite tofu restaurant. She's trying. 'Thanks anyway.'

I've always wanted to go to India. I don't know why I haven't. I could get a better yoga qualification, in a proper ashram. Or take a cooking course. I imagine riding a bicycle through back-country lanes, dodging chickens and cows, smiling at the locals with my smattering of broken Hindi. They'd offer a floor to sleep on, near where they pound the rice, and I'd work in the fields with them and keep the same hours, up with the sun, asleep with the moon because kerosene for lamps is expensive. I would find a small shrine and centre myself before it and after weeks of prayer and thought, I would find my purpose. I would stay, working for a local charity, living among the people, finding peace. There, it would be natural to be vegan. Here I look around and see people smiling while they gnaw the warm flesh of sentient beings and sometimes I think I am trapped on a planet of monsters.

'It's a short operation. No fuss. Besides, I'm too young and beautiful to be an auntie.'

'I know.'

'I'm being ironic.'

'You are beautiful.'

'I'm not beautiful and I'm not fishing.'

And there's Craig. I don't know whether it's more wrong to tell him or not. It seems unfair to burden him when the band is just beginning to take off. Yet it's sexist to assume he wouldn't want to know. Pandering to the pathetic stereotyping of young men as self-centred and irresponsible. What if he wanted to know his child, doesn't he have a right? He didn't choose this, though. With his talent, he has a remarkable life ahead of him. I don't want to be unfair.

I squeeze my eyes closed and try to imagine him carrying a baby in a sling around his chest, sitting on the floor and playing like my father used to. The image will not come. I imagine us married, living in a Californian bungalow with a trampoline and a dog and a bathroom with four different fragrances fighting each other. Buying wheat and sugar cereal from Coles. The image will not come.

'Your body, your choice.'

I rub the bridge of my nose.

'That's what our feminist foremothers fought for.'

All this time and I've done nothing. I've achieved nothing. I've been running down the years of my life. Teaching yoga, trying to help people all day in the shop, spending nights in pubs listening to music I don't like, doing a million inconsequential things.

'It's very common. Lots of women have had them. Millions. No one talks about it because of this ancient gender-loaded taboo, that's all. Men aren't judged by the same standards. No one asks a man if a foetus of theirs has been aborted.'

'Stanzi. Shut up.'

She shuts up. She sits behind the wheel, arms outstretched like she's in the middle of a long drive, eyes straight ahead, both of us going nowhere. Through the windscreen, the sky is almost dark. I wind down my window and rest my hand against the bottom of my throat and that's when I feel my mother's pendant, on its chain around my neck. I must have slipped it on before I rode over to Stanzi's.

On the footpath on the other side of the road, an older woman is walking a small white dog. She steps off the footpath as a boy passes on a bicycle. He's very late, out riding his bike alone. Probably he lives close, probably his parents know where he is. Everyone is going about their lives oblivious to what's happening to me. I don't know if I can bear to disappoint my father. And I can't think about the money it takes to raise a child, money I don't have. I think of this house, my parents and their home, the age they are now, all they've given me. I would have to move back to my old room with a baby. I don't think I can do that to either of us.

'Right. Shutting up. I thought you'd appreciate some advice. I'm trained, you know. I'm a professional.'

'I do appreciate it.'

'Because I don't need to do this. I've got better things to do than sit in a car outside Uncle Frank's place.'

'What things, exactly? What have I taken you away from?'

She bites her bottom lip. 'Well. Nothing right this second. But I could have had something.'

'I know that, Stanzi. Of course.'

'I have a busy life. I don't sit home every night waiting for you to come around and tell me you're pregnant. Next Thursday night I'm going to a seminar. Ergonomic office design. I'm almost sure my chair's too low.'

'I appreciate that you're here with me.'

'I'm not out every night bonking some no-talent hippy guitarist, that's for sure.'

'He's a bassist.' I take a deep breath. 'Right. We're going in.'

———+———

No one answers when we ring the bell, so Stanzi calls and knocks on the door. Finally we hear Uncle Frank yell *coming, coming*, then it takes a while for him to look through the peephole and undo all the locks and then the security door.

'What's wrong?' He opens the door an inch. 'What is it?'

'Nothing.' Stanzi gives me a sharp look that says *see the trouble you've caused?* 'Nothing's wrong.'

'Kip! Annabel! The girls are here! There must be some emergency!'

'An emergency!' We hear Dad yell from the lounge room. 'What is it? What's wrong?'

'No emergency, Uncle Frank,' says Stanzi. 'We thought we'd make it a family affair.'

When we finally gain admittance through Uncle Frank's wall of fluster, we follow him down the hall to the lounge. Uncle Frank doesn't own a couch or a lounge chair. Along one wall facing the TV are four cherry-red recliners that take up the whole space, the kind where the footrest swings up when you pull a lever on the side. Why he has four, I have no idea. Perhaps waiting for a wife and kids who never came. Along another wall he has two purple bean bags in a puddle. Mum and Dad are sitting in a recliner each, still wearing their coats and scarves because Uncle Frank believes heating should be saved for special occasions. Their legs are swung up so they are V-shaped, balancing on their bottoms with the soles of their feet in the air like *paripurna navasana*. In their angled laps, they each have a teacup. We both bend down to kiss Dad.

'What's wrong?' says Mum. She struggles to sit up straighter without spilling her tea. 'What is it?'

'Can't we drop around and see Uncle Frank?' says Stanzi. 'We're being good nieces.'

'They're good nieces, Annabel,' says Dad. 'They're dropping in to say hello.'

'Dropping in unexpected! That's just like you two. The blokes at Rotary were almost grandfathers by the time you two arrived. I kept saying to your father, no babies yet? And then

114

you two arrived after we'd all given up. Let me look at you both! More beautiful every day. Take after your mother. We've eaten. I don't have any more. I didn't know you were coming. Where's my kiss?'

We both kiss Uncle Frank. He's fragile with fine, pale skin and he smells of potato peel. 'We don't need anything,' says Stanzi.

'Besides, I cooked a roast lamb. This one won't eat lamb. Free the cows! Save the whales! I'm kidding. You're a good girl to care about things like that. Your father must have known you'd be an animal lover, from when you were born.'

'Francis,' says Dad.

'And she's beautiful. What a beautiful girl.' He pinches my cheek, like we're in a fairy tale.

'She is beautiful,' says Stanzi.

'And you! So clever. An apprentice headshrinker. Why don't you girls come around more often? I haven't seen you since our birthday. I'm too old. I'll be dead soon. Me, I love a lamb roast. If I have to die, why does some useless sheep get to live? Tell me that. I'd eat steak every day if it didn't get stuck in my dentures. Free advice. Always look after your teeth. Brush them. Floss them. I have some cream biscuits. That's it. Take it or leave it.'

'Cream biscuits. Yum,' says Stanzi.

'Cream biscuit, Annabel? Kip? They're the expensive ones, I can't remember the brand.'

Stanzi gives me a look that says *biscuits, of course.* Mum says, 'Biscuits! Lovely,' and Dad nods. Dad and Uncle Frank won't eat cake, won't even have it for their birthday: Mum uses chocolate icing to mortar together layers of shortbread then writes *Happy Birthday* in Smarties on the top.

Uncle Frank keeps talking as he shuffles to the kitchen. 'If you had called this morning I could have got some Kingstons. It's a waste when it's just me. Go on, sit, sit.' He means the beanbags. The recliners are for the grownups. The beanbags are for the kids. That's us.

'What is it, really?' whispers Mum.

Stanzi stares at the floor for a moment. 'Just drink your tea.' She lifts up one of the bean bags with two fingers. 'This looks like a enormous purple scrotum,' she says.

She drops the bean bag, folds one knee, then the other. When she reaches the floor she nestles in it with her arms around her knees. She's still in her work suit. She couldn't be more uncomfortable if she was in *padmasana* on a bed of nails.

'Charlotte? How's Craig?' says Mum.

'Well, apparently. With more get up and go than I would have imagined,' says Stanzi.

'Have you two split up? Is that why you're here, Charlotte? What is it?'

Stanzi says nothing. Dad says nothing.

'Well?'

'I need some fresh air,' I say.

I walk back along the hall, undo all the locks and step outside. I know this house. We played here often when we were very small. The front patio is fifties terrazzo, always cold regardless of the weather but quite lairy for Uncle Frank, whose love for concrete is everywhere. I remember thinking terrazzo was the ultimate evidence of the beauty of the natural world, this stone inlaid with sparkling chips of every colour. Stanzi laughed and told me it was man-made and this made me even happier. Humans can make something beautiful and useful from tiny things that would be inconsequential by themselves.

Mum doesn't like this house but Dad does. I think Dad would prefer to live near here, closer to where he grew up. Instead he sold his half to Uncle Frank and bought our house for Mum. Family house, family suburb, family man. Stanzi and I had a beautiful childhood. We were at the centre of both their lives. What they must have sacrificed, I am only now realising.

I hear someone approaching—probably Uncle Frank to rebolt all the doors—so I walk the narrow side path that separates the house from the lane. In the backyard, I look up. The shop across the lane is much bigger, more substantial, brick with a tiled roof. It looms over this little weatherboard house. Someone lives on the upper storey: in one window I can see curtains and a light. I wonder what it would be like to live above your own business, looking down on the little houses nestled in your shadow.

Some parts of the backyard have escaped the cement. There's a vegetable patch and a shed and a little way inside the fence near the corner is a huge lilly pilly. It towers over the yard and even stretches across the corner of the lane. The cement under the branches is a carpet of squashed purple fruit. I run my hands around the tree; the bark is rough on my palms and they tingle. My nose bristles from the cold. I sit on the bed of earth near the trunk. I cannot delay now, not one more second. I am being consumed and the decision must be made. I have no incense, no oils, no candles, but soon I need to go in and speak to my parents. I cannot wait.

I rub my hands together, reach around my neck to unfasten the pendant and warm it in my hands. It is perfect, purple and gold with sharp edges, the right thing to make this decision because it is part of my family. My mother gave it to me and my father gave it to her. It is my connection with all those who have gone before me.

The trough is rough against my back. The lower branches have tilted down and I feel enclosed by nature. I lift my shirt and pull down the band of my skirt a little so that my stomach is bared. I say the question over and over: should I keep the baby?

Now it is no longer my problem. I have offered it up to Gaia. The pendant will circle clockwise for yes, anti-clockwise for no. I close my eyes and raise my hand. The pendant begins to move.

CHAPTER FIVE

Francis

CRANSTON IS PRETENDING to sleep. The old mansion is dark and spooky and the only light in the bedchamber comes from the full moon that floods in through the big glass windows facing the moor. Cranston examines the surrounds with his experienced and brilliant eyes. They suspect him, he knows. That is why they've set a guard to sleep in the next bed, not for his own protection as they said last night. The guard is one of the assorted nameless goons that slink around masquerading as servants. Yet there is no choice. It must be tonight. Cranston may not get another opportunity to search the mansion.

Silence is of the extreme essence. If his country's enemies were to find him wandering about like he owns the place, looking for the top-secret room that contains the top secret stolen uranium, they would know he is not the debonair playboy adventurer he pretends to be. A chance presents itself, forthwith. The guard is a stupid, weak-willed buffoon who has failed in his duty and fallen asleep while on watch. Cranston looks at the guard, at his gormless boofy head. He lacks even the rudimentary intelligence required of a valet. Who knows what hideous crimes this oaf has committed? What violence he is capable of? Yet Cranston must seize this moment. He must move with no more sound than the wind.

He removes the bedclothes: first the blanket, then the sheet. He sits up, silently. He slides his feet into his slippers.

Wait! Is that the guard stirring?

'Francis if you get out of bed again so help me I'll brain you,' says the guard, who is clearly a drongo of the first order.

But Lamont Cranston will not be caught so easily.

'Righto. I'll piss right here in the bed, shall I? And tell Ma it was your idea?' Cranston replies, devastatingly outwitting his inferior foe. The thickheaded guard has his eyes closed and cannot see Cranston smile in victory.

'Jesus Mary and Joseph,' says the guard, adding blasphemy to his long list of character flaws. 'Your bladder must have been made in Japan.'

The guard could not be more wrong. Cranston's bladder is as good as cast-iron, the result of his superior willpower and years of training in the mysterious ways of the Far East. The guard suspects nothing. He rolls over to face the wall and Cranston escapes the bedroom and closes the door softly behind him! He is free! Serves them right. Everyone in the world should know by now—THE SHADOW CANNOT BE DEFEATED!

The huge stone corridor is pitch black and lit only by old-fashioned torches ablaze in holders attached to the wall. Cranston inches his way along, soundlessly yet manfully, on his tippy toes. He moves along the wall, avoiding the floorboard that creaks third from the end.

Then I see it. The kitchen. The cakes.

———✦———

The cakes have been coming for three days, ever since the funeral. On the drainer and in the cupboard and even on top of the ice box. Pound cake with butter, jam roly-poly, cinnamon tea cake, all wrapped in wax paper. We could have cake for breakfast, dinner and tea for the rest of the year. Two weeks ago this would've been heaven.

The cakes are from friends and neighbours and people from the church and mothers from school. One thing I've learned about funerals is this: even if you're not a relative, you still have to go, you have no choice in the matter, but you don't have to say anything except *a terrible thing*, over and over, as long as you shake your head and look at the ground and send over a cake. I've already got a sultana and date fruit cake with lemon icing in my bag for school today. In case anyone tries to talk about Dad and I can't think of what to say.

At the head of the kitchen table is his chair. It looks the same as the others but it's his. Was his. I run my hand along the wood, the square corner, down the slats at the back. I pull the chair out. I touch the seat, scratch my nails along the padded bit. It's brown roses like the lounge. This is where he sat, every single night. When we were little, me and Kip'd sit under the table. It was our fort. He'd sit down and say to Ma, *where the devil are those boys?* We could only see up to his knee; his shin was about our size. His socks were thick and baggy—boots left at the front door, Ma insists. We'd take it in turns to poke his ankles. Soft at first, then harder. *Jean we got mice under this table*, he'd say. *Shoo, mice.* Then he'd give a little kick and we'd scramble out of range until our giggling gave us away and he'd haul us out. *Jean this is the funniest looking pair of mice I ever saw! I'll just pop them over the back fence.* He could carry both of us, one squirming under each arm, legs kicking. When we were small.

I'm nearly thirteen and there's no one left in the world big enough to carry me under one arm. I crawl between the chairs and sit there hugging my knees and the underside of the table-top hits the back of my head and I can't believe the two of us ever fitted. I shut my eyes and imagine Dad's legs just there. Like I could touch them if I just reached out my hand.

———+———

I sleep late and when I get up I see them sitting in their usual places as if it's a usual day, as if he'll be along any second. The clock on the mantel has just gone seven. Dad would be going to work.

'Sit down,' Ma says. 'Eat something before we drown in cakes.'

I sit down in my chair and Ma gets up and opens the oven

122

and takes out a pile of scones she's wrapped in a tea towel to warm. There's jam on the table, and butter. For the life of me I can't even touch them.

'They're not going to waste,' Ma says. 'People are good enough to bring them.'

Even Kip doesn't move. Connie looks like she's going to be sick.

'I'm waiting,' Ma says.

I cut a scone in half and butter it. The butter melts like a slick. Kip takes a plain one. Connie cuts it in half and has a tiny nibble.

The butter and the jam. On the table. They've been bought with Dad's money, with his wages from the *Argus*. I don't know why I didn't think of this before.

'Ma,' I say, but I don't know how to go on with it.

'What?'

Payments on the house, wood for winter that's nearly here. What if someone gets sick and needs the doctor? Kip and I have our scholarships, but there's books and we'll both need new uniforms pretty soon. Connie's art school. Food.

'Cat got it, Francis?' Ma says.

Ma's old. Nearly as old as Dad, close to forty. If she dies too there'll just be me and Connie and Kip. I don't have the foggiest what Dad used to earn, what it costs to keep the house, but I know what happens if we can't afford to stay here in Rowena Parade. Those slum shacks in Mahoney Street, what they call the Valley of Death on account of the diphtheria. Whenever we passed it, Dad used to say there but for the grace of the *Argus* go us.

'Well?'

'What are we going to do for money?' I say.

Kip slams his fist down on the table. 'He's not been in the ground a week!' he says. Then all at once he's out of his seat, grabbing me by the collar, tipping over my chair and pulling me up and against the wall like he's going to clock me and it takes Ma and Connie to pull him off. Ma gives both of us a whack and my ear is red and stinging and ringing.

'We will all sit down like Christians or I'll give the pair of you a hiding you'll remember till this time next year.' Her mouth is that tight and white I know she'd do it. When we were little, Dad was never the one that done it. It was always her.

Connie rights my chair and we all sit and Kip is snivelling and looking at me fierce.

'If you had half a brain Kip Westaway you'd be dangerous. Your brother is, as usual, the grownup one.' Ma takes the scone from Kip's plate and puts it on mine. 'This is nobody's business but mine. But this is how it's going to be.' Ma tells us we have a little money: a collection at St Ignatius and another from St Kevin's and from the *Argus*. And tomorrow morning, she starts work.

'Not in a common factory,' she says. 'I'm to be a housemaid in a big place at Kew. Father Lockington himself arranged it. They've given me a black dress and all. And Connie. You tell them.'

'I won't go back to art school. I can get a job too.'

'A job? Not on your nelly. I won't have these two roaming the streets like urchins. We're taking in a boarder. Myrna

Keith's sister-in-law, the widow. She's a bit of money from her uncle that passed and she wants to live around here, near her relations. The boys can share a bed in our room and you can stay out in the laundry. You can look after her and the boys.'

For a while nobody says anything. Connie stirs her tea and the clink of her spoon sounds that loud.

'It'd be better if we weren't at school. Wouldn't it, Ma?' says Kip.

'Well you are at school and that's that. Brother Cusack had a word at the funeral. The scholarships keep going till you finish if you keep your marks up, and the brothers'll find whatever books you need, and uniforms, and anything else. After that, who knows? Three boys that finished last year went on to the university. You're too young to leave school besides.'

'You can get an exemption certificate from the government. Trudy Lee is thirteen and she got one and now she's at the match factory.'

Ma's throat is red. I wonder if she's scratched it by accident but her nails are that short I don't know how she'd do it. She gives Kip a look that means *one more word and I'll knock you into the middle of next week* but instead she says, 'Respectable people keep their children on at school. Your father, he gave up everything for us. That's that.'

The three of us look at each other. We know the story word for word, mostly because when Connie was little she'd be at Ma all the time. *Tell it again, Ma, tell it again.* Like it was the greatest romance ever, better even than a film. Dad's people were of a different persuasion and didn't approve and wouldn't even come to St Ignatius for the wedding, and that's how come we don't know our grandparents and aunties and uncles from that side. All Father Donovan asked, Ma says, was that we were brought up Catholic and went to Catholic school and Dad gave his word. Even though Dad never came to St Ignatius with us, every Sunday he made us go. Until you're old enough to decide on your own, he'd say.

'Happy now, you pair of worry warts?'

We nod, but happy doesn't come in to it. My scone is still lying there, slit up the middle. Kip keeps looking at it like he's never seen a scone before. Connie is giving up art school when all she cares about is drawing pictures. Ma is going into domestic service, cleaning someone else's house. But, for me and Kip, life will be just the same as before: St Kevin's, our friends, the brothers. What's going to happen to Ma when she gets old, when Connie goes off to get married? Who's going to look after her now Dad's gone? That's what I'd like to know.

———————+———————

Today will be the hardest. The funeral wasn't so bad. Dad looked like he was just sleeping and it was good to see everyone so sad for him, shaking me and Kip by the hand, telling us what a great bloke Dad was. At funerals everyone has a job to do and things happen all by themselves. As if we were all in a play and everyone knew their lines.

Back to school, that's what I've been dreading. Boys and brothers and everyone looking at me from the corners of their eyes. One thing I've learned: when your father dies, people are much kinder to you. For a while, anyway.

This will be Cranston's most difficult assignment yet, indisputable proof of his genius. He's practised for this, like a cricketer playing his first test. *Thank you for your sympathy, Brother. I'm feeling much better, thank you.*

Cranston goes to his room to get his bag. The target isn't there, but it's much too early for him to have left already. Where the blazes is he?

'Ma, have you seen Kip?'

'He left ten minutes ago. I told you not to dawdle.'

Bugger. The target has thrown off the tail. I bolt out the front door, along Rowena Parade, down Lennox Street. Usually we catch the tram along Swan to the MacRobertson Bridge but it's that early, odds are Kip's decided to walk. I cut through Gipps Street then Elm Grove walking fast but there's no sign of him. Then, as I come around the corner into Mary Street, I see them: the evil Mastermind Shiwan Khan and his two goons, leaning on a fence, smoking.

'Francis,' nods Jim Pike.

'Have you seen Kip? I've lost him.'

Pike looks up at the sun and squints and purses his lips, but can't hold in his giggle. The other two start to laugh as well.

'Bad couple of weeks you're having, Francis. If you've lost your brother as well,' he says.

'Yeah,' says Cray, and all three of them laugh all the harder.

'Francis, Francis, come here, matey,' says Pike. He's a good head taller than me and rangy: big, but not as big as Cray or Mac. They're both like a cross between a brick dunny and a gorilla and Mac takes after the gorilla in the body-hair department. Pike vices one arm around my shoulders. 'Me and the lads are just having a joke with you. We're sorry to hear about your dad. Aren't we, boys.'

'Yeah,' says Cray.

'Real sorry,' says Mac. He comes over and pulls back his fist like he's going to punch me into the middle of next week, but instead when it lands he takes all the force out of it and he just taps my arm.

'Ta.' I think about the sultana cake in my bag, try to calculate its anti-bashing value. It was meant for school but I'll spend it now if I have to.

'In fact, we been thinking. Might be you could hang about with us for a bit.' Pike lets go of me and leans back against the wall.

I swallow. I look at him.

'We've been keeping an eye on you Frankie,' says Mac. 'We could use a lad of your talents.'

Really? 'What talents would those be?'

'You're smart and hardworking,' says Pike, which is true. 'Sometimes, the boys and me, we make a bit of pocket money doing odd jobs for old ladies out in Hawthorn. Gardening and such. Our good deeds to help the less fortunate.'

This makes Mac smile from ear to ear. 'We call it our charitable works.' Cray starts laughing so hard he doubles over and puts his hands on his knees.

'We think you'd be the ideal boy to join our gang,' says Pike.

'What about,' I start. 'Thought you blokes prefer to stick with your own kind.'

'Your religion,' says Mac. 'In this instance we're prepared to overlook it.'

'All right, then.'

'Start today after school,' says Mac. 'And don't say nothing to nobody. One word and it's all off. Once you're friends with us—well, let's just say. It's best to be friends with us.'

'Friends with us is the best way to be,' says Pike, and he's right about that. 'So shut your cakehole.'

'Not a word.'

'Back here, straight after the bell,' Pike says. I nod.

———————✦———————

After they leave, I lean for a while against the heat of the wall and think about my luck. The toughest gang in Richmond! And they want me, Francis Westaway! All right, I'm not as big as them. I'm not as muscly. But I'm wiry, and more to the point, I'm sharp. Give it time, I could be the brains of the whole operation. Officer in charge of all charitable works. They've noticed my potential, the big life I've got in front of me. No more handing over sandwiches, getting tripped, watching where I sit and where I walk. Could be I've been hung from my feet to the hilarity of all and sundry to have my pockets emptied for the last time. Dackings? Forget it. From now on, I'll be the one doing the dacking. From this minute it'll be me deciding who does what and who goes where. Francis, is it all right if I sit here? Francis would you like a biscuit? No, no, go on. It's the last one in the packet, but you have it.

When I get to school I hunt for Kip from one end to the other, in all his usual spots. Then I remember: the library. Sure enough when I peek through the window I can see him. He's sitting on the floor in the corner, but he's not reading. He's hugging his knees and his head is down. Looking at him there, I forget why I was chasing him.

'If we told the boys we had scones for breakfast, they'd not believe us,' I say, when I sit beside him.

He looks up. It takes him a long time to move his head, like it's extra heavy. 'Did you see that scone? Split up the middle like that?'

I nod.

'That's what they did to his suit coat. His good suit coat. Cut up the back.'

'They never. How do you know a thing like that?'

'It wasn't sitting right. I could see, when I was standing in front of the coffin. The collar didn't line up properly. Didn't join. I expect they did it to his shirt as well.'

The bell goes: I can hear it echoing against the walls and ceilings and stairs. We're supposed to be in class quick smart. History. Yet we're both sitting here on the floorboards, backs against the rows of books, calm as you like. Gentlemen of leisure, Ma would say. Kip ignores the bell. Or maybe he doesn't hear it.

'What do you suppose they cut it with?'

'Scissors, maybe. Or a knife. He'd be that mad,' said Kip. 'That was his best coat. It's a wonder Ma let them.'

'No other way to get his arms in, I expect.'

130

Kip shakes his head. 'No excuse for it. You'd do it the way Connie used to dress her dolls. Just takes patience, that's all. I can't bear the thought of it. Him lying there forever with his best clothes slit open at the back.'

It seems to me that Dad's beyond caring about clothes, but I don't say that to Kip. He's making his hands into fists and if he knew who'd cut Dad's clothes they'd be getting what for.

'We'd best get moving. Rise and Fall of the Roman Empire.'

'I'm not going. I thought I could but I can't.'

Kip's hair is in his eyes. It takes so little effort to keep your fringe trimmed. Ma's happy to do it, he just has to ask. But Kip's just like Dad that way; he always used to come home with ink under his fingernails. Outside in the hall, I can hear boys and brothers hurrying to class, doors shutting. Everywhere else, women are going to the shops and men are off to work and derros are sitting in the park and none of them give a rat's about Dad.

'The first day's the hardest,' I say. 'All downhill from here.'

'I didn't even say goodbye to him, that morning. I was reading a stupid book.'

Dad and me and Connie, we all laugh at the way Kip reads a book. You could talk right at him. You could sprinkle water on his head and drop a saucepan lid next to him and he'd not look up. *Read through an earthquake*, Dad used to say.

'He knew that's how you are,' I say. 'It's how you've always been.'

'Did you not bloody well hear me? I didn't say goodbye to Dad. On account of a book.'

'You've got to get to class. It's not up to you. Ma says you're staying.'

He stands. He doesn't pick up his bag: just leaves it lying on the floor.

'What can she do? She can't kill me.'

'She bloody can.' I can tell from the set of his jaw he's not joking. 'What will you do?'

He shrugs. 'If the factories won't take me I'll go door to door. I'll do anything.' He looks down at me, blinking fast, squeezing his eyes tight then opening them wide. 'Rise and Fall of the bloody Roman Empire. Us sitting there like good little boys at our good little desks. *Yes brother, no brother*, when he's dead and he's never coming home and I never even said a proper goodbye.'

I want to tell him he's not being practical, that he needs to think of his future, of Ma's and Connie's. I want to tell him Dad would understand. Instead I say, 'Piker.'

He kicks his bag on the floor and makes straight for the door and doesn't say goodbye and I know he's heading for Brother Cusack's room. His bag is lying there where he left it. I don't know what to do with it. All I can think is how silly I'll look to the gang if I turn up with two schoolbags. In the end, I leave it there on the floor.

———+———

After the last bell, I walk down the stairs as fast as I can. Kip never appeared for history, or for maths after that. None of the brothers spoke to me about him. I expect they'll give it a few days, give him a chance to change his mind. They don't know him like I do. It makes me extra glad I have somewhere to go this afternoon because with Kip and Ma, home will be a good place not to be. Some of the other boys try to stop me but I tell them I've got to see man about a dog and I rush past. I can't let them slow me down. I can't be late at the very beginning. I don't know how long the gang will wait.

But when I get back to the wall in Mary Street, they're not there. Maybe I got the place or the time wrong, or they're not going to come at all and it's their idea of a big jape. And then I see them turn the corner, walking casual as you like, with bags over their shoulders.

I lean on the wall straightaway. I nod.

'Hope we haven't kept you waiting, Frankie,' says Jim.

'Just got here. Thought the brothers might of kept me back.'

'What for?' says Mac.

I look to the heavens. 'Where do I start? All the trouble I get into.'

'I knew you'd fit right in Frankie,' says Jim. 'Let's go.'

We walk down to Swan Street and I go to get on the tram but I see the boys hanging back. They wait until it's going again and they run after it and jump on the ledge at the back. Just like that. On the back, hanging on. They're looking at each other and grinning. Pike takes one arm off the rail and waves at me. *Come on*, he mouths. And I've got one second to make up my mind and all I can think about is Dad but then I think about Kip walking out of school and I'm not walking away from anything so I run after them and I jump on too.

I don't think about it, from then on. Because if I did fall off, my head would crack like an egg and because it's busy with people and even cars everywhere, not late at night like when Dad did it, I'd probably be run over and end up a big red splodge on the road and they'd slice my coat from the collar down so I hang on sweaty and shaking and keep not thinking about it. All the people on the street stop and stare at us and one man takes off his hat and waves it and yells *Hoy! You boys!* Cray waves back at him with one arm and I keep gripping on with two and not thinking.

'No sense wasting good money on a ticket,' says Jim.

'Optional,' says Cray.

'Simple economics,' says Mac. 'You all right there, Frankie?'

I can feel every grain of sand on the track. My hands are greasy and slipping. Near the turn into Power Street the tram slows to walking speed and we jump off and my legs are that wobbly I can hardly stand. We walk for a bit but then another tram comes along. This time the connie's looking at us something fierce so we get on and buy our tickets and I've never been so happy in my life.

So we're standing in the middle of the tram as it squeaks and rattles. When we get to Hawthorn you can tell the difference right away. Hawthorn is grass and swaying trees and hills and houses that don't even touch each other but have grass the whole way around like a moat. Even the air has a different smell. We hop off near the Burwood Road corner and walk around the side of a milk bar behind a big tree, and then we stop. Before I know what's going on, I see Mac undoing his buttons. The three of them are taking off their

134

shirts, right down to their white singlets, right there. And I look at Mac, at the hair under his arms sticking out a good three inches! Even a few tufts on his chest. I hope to high heaven I don't have to take my shirt off. I look like I've been dipped in toffee. From their school bags, they each pull out a plain shirt and cap.

When I ask why they're changing, Cray starts to laugh.

'I'm surprised you need to ask that question, Frankie,' says Jim. 'Our poor mothers slave day and night doing the washing. When we're out working hard in old ladies' yards our shirts get awful filthy. We don't want to dirty our school clothes like that.'

'Thoughtless,' says Cray.

That's good thinking on the boys' behalf. I've only got the one suit for school myself. 'Oh. Where's mine?'

Cray has a mighty giggle at that.

'You don't need one,' says Jim. 'We're all bigger than you, see? Stronger. It's best that me and Cray and Mac do the yard work. We're saving you for a part of the job that needs a bit more thought. A special bit. You being so good at school and that.'

Well, there you are. I knew they'd picked me for good reason. Brains not brawn, that's what counts. They're saving me for a special bit.

'And cause you're so weedy,' says Mac.

After we walk for a while, we come to a big house with a lot of yard, all covered with bushes and grass and trees run amuck. No wonder the lady who lives here needs help with her garden. I start to open the gate but Mac grabs me and

135

pulls me back to the footpath and over in front of the house next door.

'Listen carefully. This is what's going to happen. The old dear inside, she's expecting us.'

'Righto.' I start to move again but Cray puts his hand on my chest.

'But not all of us. Just Mac and Cray and me. You stay here till she lets us in. Then we make sure the door isn't locked behind us, right? She'll take us through the house and into the backyard and show us what to cut back and what weeds to pull. That's when you get to it.'

'Get to it?'

'Start with the kitchen,' says Pike. 'And only bother with the small stuff.'

'Big stuff's no good, in case we got to leg it,' says Mac. 'No matter if you want it or not. Even if it's, I dunno, a wireless. If it doesn't fit in your pocket, leave it.'

'Pocket size,' says Cray.

'Money, jewellery,' says Pike. 'These old ducks, they don't like banks. Look in her drawers, under her smalls. That's where they keep purses.'

'Jewellery. What do we want with jewellery?'

'It's not for us, you idiot,' says Pike. 'It's for flogging. My brother Ronnie shifts it down the pub.'

'In the kitchen, check the tea caddy,' says Mac. 'Sometimes there're pound notes in there to pay delivery boys.'

'Most important of all: eyes and ears open,' says Pike. 'We'll keep her in the backyard as long as we can but you can never tell when they get it in their head to get you a glass of water or something. If you hear a sound, go straight out the front door.'

'We'll meet back at the milk bar,' says Mac. 'Everything gets split four ways.'

'And Francis.' Pike looks at me closely. 'Don't disappoint us. You wouldn't like us when we're disappointed.'

'Yeah,' says Cray.

———+———

From his advantage point behind the front fence, Cranston watches the big old door of the castle open with a ginormous screech. Just as he planned, his agents—three hirsute former convicts whose miserable lives The Shadow has saved and who owe him plenty and have sworn eternal fealty for the rest of their existence—say the secret password and gain admittance to the villains' hideout. Now is his chance to search for the stolen microfilm. He leaves his bag with the others, tucked just inside the gate. When he reaches the door, it is ajar. He opens it without a word and slips into the foyer.

Inside it is dark and musty, as though the super-villains for whom this is their lair don't own a broom. When his eyes adjust to the light, he sees a number of rooms coming off a central corridor, which is lined with suits of armour and rugs that Cranston knows originate in a small village outside Constantinople. But this is no time to dawdle and reflect on his adventures in the Ottoman Empire. Cranston's ticker is hammering so loud he's scared it'll give the game away, but he's got to step on it. The villains might return at any moment.

He starts in the kitchen, a tiny dirty room designed for servants or perhaps the villains' mothers. He checks the tea caddy as per the tip off but as he suspected from the rundown and shabby appearance of the castle, it holds only tea and a few pennies. In case they are useful as clues, he scoops the pennies into his pocket. He looks in all the other containers too: F for flour and S for sugar. They are all but empty. The fruit bowl is empty. The bread bin is empty. There's not enough food in here for a mouse watching her figure. What is wrong with this old biddy? There's shops just at the end of the street and if it's too far to walk, the grocer's boy'll bring it.

Cranston figures that this room is a waste of time and all the while he searches he keeps an ear out for noise. If he's found, it's extreme curtains for our handsome hero.

Next, he checks the front room. Here he must be careful: he can tell by one look at the mantel that everything is covered in a fine layer of fingerprint dust and if he touches anything he's had it. In a brilliant bit of ingenuity he slips his sleeves down over his fingers while he checks behind photo frames and a big clock but there's nothing small enough to fit in his pocket. There are distant noises of his agents' voices. They are excellent distractors. He has taught them well.

Finally he makes his way to the villains' old-lady house-keeper's room. At first he just stands at the door. It's like being at his nan's: a big high bed with a hollow in the middle and flat lace cushions instead of pillows. There are slippers on the floor and a white nightie on a chair. The whole room smells of old lady. Cranston looks along the dresser and rifles through some drawers. Everything is faded and thin. There is no microfilm here. He feels sick. He thinks for a moment he's going to hurl.

Then, all at once, he hears a noise. It's talking. Loud. Yelling, getting closer. There's another noise—it's the back door opening. He's nearly shat himself. They're coming in the back door. He can hear them, clomping boys' feet and the old lady too. Bugger bugger bugger. Perhaps they're just stopping in the kitchen for a drink. That's it. No. They're coming closer, right along the hall, up to the front.

I nip behind the bedroom door and pull it back towards me and straightaway a dressing-gown flutters in my face and it smells of dried sick and tea. They're in the hall, outside the bedroom door. I can hardly breathe. I'm trapped.

'But we've only just started,' says Pike. 'We don't want to quit yet.'

'Anyway,' says Mac, 'it's for free.'

'He pulled out a rhododendron,' the old lady says.

'We'll be more careful.'

'Honest.'

'You lot wouldn't know a weed if it came up and shook you by the hand. You're good for nothing.'

'Give us another chance,' says Pike.

'You're like elephants in a china shop. You should be paying me for elementary gardening instruction.'

I can't see a thing with my head behind the dressing-gown but I can feel something solid resting on my cheek. I pull aside the gown and hanging next to it on the a hook at the back of the door is a black handbag. I take it down. Quietly I open the rusty clasp. Inside there's a hankie, a gold lipstick and matching compact and a fat leather purse. I empty the purse into my hand: a fistful of shillings. I stuff them in my pocket.

'Oh. Oh. Did somebody turn out the lights?' says Pike. 'I feel dizzy. I think I'm having a fainting spell.'

'Strewth,' says Cray.

'Mother? Mother, is that you?' says Pike.

'It's the sun, I expect,' says Mac. 'Heatstroke.'

'You were in the sun all of five minutes,' the old lady says.

'My friend is of a sensitive disposition,' says Mac.

'Are you some kind of foreigner?' she says.

'Can I have a drink?'

'Water. You're not getting my lemonade when you've done naught to earn it.'

I can hear her tramping back up the hall, and then Pike whispers, 'Francis. Where the bloody hell are you?'

I come out from behind the dressing-gown. The old lady's in the kitchen. I can hear the clink of glasses, water sloshing in a sink, but I'm not thinking about that. I freeze in the middle of the bedroom. I think about Ma. Her and the old lady aren't that different. I haven't looked in the most obvious place.

In a flash I dart to the bed and shove my hand under the mattress. I feel around and around and then the back of my hand touches something soft and furry, like velvet. I pull it out—it's a small red bag a couple of inches square, with a gold drawstring pulled tight. She'll be back down the hall in one more second. I go to put the bag in my pocket but I stop. I try to think like The Shadow, so instead I bend down and pop it inside my left pushed-down sock. Then I run out the bedroom door and stand behind Cray in the hall. Just then she comes around the corner from the kitchen.

She's walking down the hall, rolling a little from side to side, glass of water in her hand. She's spilled some on the carpet, she doesn't care. She stops in front of us. She's bigger than I expected, a round nan-type, not a scrawny one. Her grey hair is plastered down at the front like Julius Caesar. She squints.

'Which one of you wanted the water?'

Pike takes it off her and drains it in one scull.

'That's better. Ta. Well. We'll be off.'

We turn and Cray opens the door.

'Just wait one minute,' she says. 'Turn around.'

We don't know what to do. We turn. We stand there, the four of us in a row. I can feel the blood draining from my hands. There's a strange metallic taste in my mouth. I will be branded a juvenile delinquent. Ma will know and Connie will know and Kip will know. Brother Cusack will know. I'll be the one leaving school, that's for sure. There goes my future. There goes my famous life as a radio star.

The old lady looks us up and down and I see what this is. This is a test. This is about me sitting at the table this morning while Ma talked about her job and Connie talked about leaving school and I never said anything. Right here and now, I make a pledge to Jesus. If I get out of this alive, I will shoulder the responsibility for this family. I will work hard at school. I will be the most serious, most studious, most hard-working boy and I'll do whatever Ma says and I'll never do another naughty thing, not ever, not if I live to be a hundred.

I'll be the best boy who ever lived. I'll finish school and go to university and I'll study the law so help me Jesus Christ who is my Saviour. Ma is right: nothing is as important as being respectable. I can see the old woman's head nodding. She's counting us. It doesn't matter how old she is, everyone knows the difference between three boys and four. We've had it.

'Which is the stupid boy who pulled out my new rhododendron?'

I look at Pike and Pike looks at Mac and Mac looks at Cray.

'Me,' says Cray.

'Damages.' She holds out her fat hand.

'What?' says Pike.

'You'll be paying for that. That was a cutting from my sister-in-law's Marchioness of Lansdowne what won a ribbon at the show. Plants like that don't grow on trees.'

'Got any money?' says Pike.

Cray turns out both pockets. Pike does the same, and Mac. Two bottle caps, three bulls-eyes with lint stuck to them, a pencil stub and six marbles.

'Here.' I pull the money from my pockets, the handful of coins from the tea caddy and the purse.

The old woman stands in front of me and looks me square in the face. She leans right down so her nose is nearly touching the coins. My hand is wet with sweat. My heart actually stops, I'm sure of it. I can feel the empty space in my chest and any second my ribs are going to collapse on top of this huge cavity where my heart used to be. How can she identify a handful of coins? Has she memorised the look of the money? Perhaps she's not a little old lady after all. Perhaps she's a policeman in disguise. There could be coppers everywhere in this old house, hiding behind the couch, standing in the bath. Slowly she straightens up. She looks me right in the eye.

'Wait here. Wait till I get my glasses. You might be due some change.'

'It's fine,' I say. 'Take it. Take it all.'

———————

'"It's fine",' says Pike, in a mincing falsetto, hands clasped to his chest.

'"Take it, take it all",' says Mac, lips pursed and eyes fluttering.

'Westaway, I oughta thump you into the middle of next week, you cretin.'

'Yeah,' says Cray.

We are behind the milk bar and the boys are changing back into their school shirts. We've run almost all the way, flat out in the fading light. All that work, all that effort, for nothing. It's just not our lucky day. Cray is snivelling. I've got my arms folded because my hands won't stop shaking.

'Was it me who pulled out the rhododendron? Or was it me who got us out of it?'

'Get out of this,' says Mac, and I hear it before I feel it. A whump noise, like meat hitting a lino floor. Then I feel the pain in my nose and cheek and jaw, then I see I'm lying sideways on the grass. It takes me a moment to figure how I got on the grass. I can't see anything. My face hurts. The shop,

143

the trees are blending together. I move my head so I can look up with the other eye, the one currently pointing down at the grass. Mac's holding one hand in the other armpit, cursing and grimacing and jumping on one leg.

'Yeah,' says Cray.

I look up: he's standing square above me and before I can say no Cray please, I see him pull back one foot and I know it's coming and a second takes a minute then I feel the kick, hard, right in the guts.

I'm dying. I can't breathe. I try and be sick but it's just spit that comes up. There's red on the grass, blood. I get on my knees and lift up one hand. It's from my nose. The blood is coming out my nose and it won't stop. I'm a goner. I feel like hurling again.

My head is down low then Pike kneels beside me and grabs a fistful of my hair and yanks my head back so I think for a minute I'm going to drown in the blood from my nose that's pouring down my throat.

'This is nothing compared with the accident that's going to befall you if you say one word.'

I can hardly speak. It's like I'm gargling. He lets go of my hair and my head falls down again and I spit and cough.

'If you see us coming, Westaway, turn and go the other way,' says Mac.

I collapse back on the grass and look up at the three of them. Cray spits straight at me: I feel it land wet on my throat. I close my eyes and wait and then I open them a smidge. They're gone. I wait longer, but there's no one else here.

The sun is down and my face is hot and throbbing and I've

got to find my way home yet. Standing is quite an operation. I hold on to a lamp post with my arms. I take a step, then another. Hands out to my side so I don't go A over T. Then one foot feels funny, like the ankle won't bend right. It's not bad enough I've had a shellacking that's pulverised my face that I have to explain to Ma and that'll be a story and a half, but I've hurt my foot as well, sprinting away from the old lady's house.

I reach down to my ankle and that's when I feel it. The little bag from under her bed. I open it and under the street light I see a purple jewel hanging on a gold chain. It's a beaut, the prettiest thing I've ever seen. It sparkles under the light. I smile, and cry out loud my face hurts that much. There's no way I'm sharing this. It's mine.

CHAPTER SIX

Annabel

THE *WOMEN'S WEEKLY* says mock sausages are delicious. I boil the oats for fifteen minutes in salted water, chop the onion and add the spices and egg and bread-crumbs. The mixture sticks to the spoon, the bowl, my hands. It smells faintly of Christmas pudding. I mould it in the shape of fat beef bangers, fry them in the last of our dripping. They spit and hiss like cats. When they turn dark brown I take them from the pan but they look like no sausage I can recall. The *Women's Weekly* says they make an ideal luncheon to delight the whole family. Yesterday I made mock duck: onion, tomato, beaten egg and dried herbs, all mixed together and spread on toast. The *Women's Weekly* said it was a tasty and nutritious sandwich filling.

I've a bone to pick with the *Women's Weekly*.

My father sits in the front room waiting to be called to lunch, already halfway through his third bottle. On the plates, the mock sausages are hot but the dripping is congealing. One end of the kitchen table is set for the two of us and the other end is covered with things that don't belong there: the *Herald*, the empty fruit bowl, some candles in case the power goes off, the tea towels I've been folding. I'll move everything after we've eaten. It's only when the table's set and we're sitting that I can't bear the empty space. One of these days I'll get rid of the other two chairs. Or I'll sell this whole setting and buy a table for two.

'What are we mocking today?' In the kitchen, he pours another glass. The whole kitchen smells of it: yeasty and almost sweet.

'Guess.'

He prods a sausage with his fork. 'Some kind of meat? Maybe we should draw the curtain.' He smiles. 'Don't want the neighbours to dob us in.'

It's another week before I can buy more sugar and we're down to half a cup of tea and a scrape of butter. We're out of pepper but that can't be bought because the only countries that thought to grow it couldn't get out of the way of the Japanese. We have our own potatoes and onions and Elsie next door gives us a quarter of a pumpkin when she cuts one. The war is over and we won. Or so they say.

'Mock chutney?' I pass him the last remaining cut-crystal bowl. It belonged to my mother. The mock chutney sits in a gluggy pile and has already formed a skin. He takes a big spoonful. His enthusiasm makes me sad. Glistening and oozing, the mock chutney looks strangely like a mix of Worcestershire sauce, apricot jam and raisins.

My father slathers a hunk of sausage. He chews slowly. In all the years I've cooked for him, he's never failed to pay due attention.

'Tastes like Worcestershire sauce, apricot jam and raisins,' he says.

'You, sir, can choose any prize from the top shelf.'

He draws a long draught of beer and I watch his Adam's apple move up and down. He fills the glass again from the tall brown bottle in the middle of the table. The glass is sweating from the cold of the beer and I can see the mark where his hand has been.

'Very tasty. You're a good girl, Annabel.' And he smiles again. I've never seen the likeness, despite what people say. My great aunts recall how handsome he was as a young man, how much in love my parents were. I've seen it myself in the wedding photograph beside his bed: his shining face, smile like a hearth on a cold day. I've stared and stared at that photo. I can't see anything of my mother in me.

'You don't have a few bob to spare, love?'

I harden my heart. 'This grand sausage feast was the last of the housekeeping.' I wave my hand across the table, a magician revealing her art.

We both look down at our plates. He feels the shame of asking; me, of lying. Maybe he knows, maybe he doesn't. I've put so little aside it's hardly worth hiding. A few coppers to get us through the week. Next week will have to worry about itself. At least it's November now, heating up fast. I only need enough wood for cooking. It was different when I was in the munitions factory, before the men came home and we girls got our marching orders. Even if I could get a job now, without me here to watch him he'd likely drink what little I'd make. The fear of the Nips coming made him a better man. That's the cold fact about the war: me and Dad never had it so good.

We eat for a while in silence and I wait for the sentence that will begin it. It will likely arrive when he takes his last bite. And as I stand to put the kettle on the hob, he scrapes his plate and rests his knife and fork at six o'clock.

'Stuck here,' he says, 'looking after your old man. You should have a family of your own by now.'

'I do have a family of my own. You.'

This is our private dance, my father's and mine. We know our steps by heart. It is our own play and like good actors we say our lines with true emotion as if every time is the first. Soon he will say something about me being alone and what it costs me to care for him.

'No mother, no brothers. Working her youth away, looking after an old man. All your friends married or working.'

'I love looking after you.' I know he loves me. But some days when I hear him say *no mother, no brothers*, I think he really means *no wife, no sons*.

'It's bloody unfair,' he whispers.

Today he's resigned. He is not always so tranquil, but even then I know it's not me he's angry at. I'm just the one who's here. It's not my fault, and it's not the fault of the plates or the glasses or the walls or the furniture or what was once the set of my mother's cut-crystal bowls. Being with him on a bad day is like watching a storm break in the distance. It seems so far away that I am untouched, I am calm inside. But surely it would be better if I felt something.

Today is a good day. He drains his Melbourne Bitter. He doesn't have to say a word; I am perfectly trained. I fetch another bottle. I serve the main meal in the middle of the day. Small adjustments for the reality of our situation: my father never takes a drop before noon.

'If only I could buy you a new dress or take you to the pictures. I'm a terrible father, Annabel.'

'You're a wonderful father, always have been.'

At this stage, he's still calling me Annabel. I have my tea and we sit and talk about this and that, neighbourhood things, the line-up of Saturday's team, and after the sixth bottle he goes to stand, both palms flat on the table top. The chair clatters over behind him, so that's good. If he can stand by himself it's easier. When he goes out in his chair it's very hard to move him—once he went while he was still eating, face forward, nose-first into the mash.

Another time he made it all the way through lunch and went to fetch something from the bedroom. It was a dark day, raining outside, and the blinds were drawn and I found him passed out on the floor, gasping and gagging, a trail of dark liquid running from his mouth. I opened his mouth and my fingers felt a sticky mass. His tongue, I thought. He's bitten off his tongue and he's choking on it. My fingers were wet with warm blood. I gripped the slippery glob and pulled it out and forced myself to look at it. It took a moment for my eyes to

151

adjust, and when they did I saw it was a toffee. A toffee! He must've shoved it in his mouth just before hitting the deck. Once it was out he could breath just fine. He lay there sleeping and I sat on the floor beside him, fingers stuck together by the half-chewed toffee and laughed until I cried.

Today, though, he stands by himself and stretches his arms out to the side. All at once he starts to wobble. I move quickly. Perhaps he'll shake off my arm and say he'll be fine and yell *what do you think I am, some kind of cripple, get away, I can manage.* His hands are slow and easy to dodge.

'Here, Dad.' I move the fallen chair aside and lift one of his arms around my shoulder and bend a little so we're snug. He doesn't say a word. I'm practised at this. Oh, there was one Thursday night I lost the balance of him altogether and we careened into the hall table and broke the lamp and the vase and he cut his head and I twisted my ankle. I lay there among the broken bits and blood and him sleeping like an angel and I thought, how the devil am I going to get him up now?

That was when I thought sleeping in the hallway was a disaster. These days I'm stronger and he's thinner and I've learned to lean on the walls while I change my grip and to use his arm as a pivot.

I doubt I'd drop him now but if I did I'd check for injuries then lift his head and slide a pillow under it and cover him with a blanket and leave him. Now I know there are worse things than sleeping on the floor.

Today is easy. I use my hips and my legs and my shoulders. We are like slow runners in a three-legged race. We pass the hall table with no trouble, take the corner of the front room with ease. His chair is ready, just as he left it. This can be the hardest part. I need to line him up exactly. I take both his hands, a moment's pause—and there it is. He falls like a tree but the chair holds him and it is not yet four o'clock. I have time to get ready.

I am almost out of the room when I hear him mumble.

'Are you going out, Meg?'

'Yes, Dad.' He knows who I am all right. It's just that when he's like this, my mother's name is still the easiest to find.

'Where?'

'For a walk, maybe along the river. Then afterwards to a dance.'

'Picking you up?'

'In half an hour.'

'Won't be late?'

'No, Dad. I won't be late.'

Then my father opens one eye and it looks clear and sharp and blue, as if it belonged to someone else. 'You know I don't like that boy,' he says. 'I don't trust him.'

He has never said this before. This is not part of our act.

'Dad.' I sit on the edge of the lounge and take his hand. It is not alert like his eye; it is limp and mottled and flabby. 'That's not true. You like Francis. You told me so.'

He gives a soft snort. I've said the silliest thing. 'Not him. He's harmless. The other one. Kip.' He closes his eye and falls back to sleep.

I boil the kettle and fill the basin and there's no way I can make sense of it. I wash my face and do my hair and change into one of my mother's dresses taken in at the waist and perhaps I heard it wrong. Not one boy had called for me, ever, in my life, before Francis knocked on our door one Sunday afternoon. I've got Dad, he's got me. We do just fine on our own.

Francis is different from the other Richmond blokes. He stands straighter, holds his mouth firmer. He makes the rest of them seem like kids; he's close to perfect and even I can't stain him. He's been taking me out for the best part of six months but I've known him since I was a schoolgirl.

I've met Kip barely a dozen times since he's been out of the army; Dad's met him just once or twice. Kip is perfectly nice. Not as handsome as Francis on account of his nose, which he never got straightened the way Francis did, but fine looking. He's a photographer's assistant at the *Argus*, they put him on again as soon as he got back. Francis is a clerk in a law office: that'll set him up for the future, he says.

Francis does say things about Kip that aren't so flattering, about him being aimless and—what is it?—dreamy. I've always put that down to some kind of thing between brothers. The two of them only have each other. I've never thought there was anything wrong with Kip Westaway. I've never thought of him at all.

I'm so busy thinking I don't hear the knock at first. I look out my window: Francis is standing at the door, holding his fist up like he intends to pound it to firewood. I have to rush before he ruins everything.

'I thought there was no one home,' he says. 'Where were you? Never mind. Let's go inside for a bit. Sit down. I wouldn't mind a quick word with your father.'

'Dad's asleep.' I slip outside and close the door behind us.

Along the river, not far from the Botanic Gardens, there are lots of couples walking. They all walk like us: slowly, the man slightly in front, no touching. Francis's hands are in his pockets. In Paris couples might stroll arm in arm, but this is Melbourne.

Francis points to a seat further up the bank. 'Let's sit for a while.' He charges up the hill. I follow.

On the other side of Punt Road, back across the river, I can see Richmond but here in South Yarra there are trees and birds and flowers and I imagine it's like the country but nicer, more polite. Tonight Francis is taking me to Leggett's, which is so posh there's even a cloakroom. Cloaks! Imagine it! Not that I'll need one tonight: it's mild and fine. Tonight there are two bands and dancing until midnight. We won't stay that long, of course. Dad usually wakes around ten. I wouldn't want him to worry.

It's a picture, here by the water. Same bit of river, yet it seems cleaner on this side. A shame Francis can't sit still long enough to enjoy it. If he's not standing to shake out the crease in his trousers, he's resting one ankle on one knee, then stretching his legs straight out or brushing at some imaginary speck of lint.

155

'What's your dad doing with himself these days?'

'The odd day at the tannery. Not so much work as there was.'

'He should get into another field. We've never been busier at McReady's. Another three contracts landed on my desk just yesterday. Good times and bad, people always need lawyers. To think I once thought about going for a job on the wireless. What a silly business.'

I think of the voices on the radio, so posh they sound English, so sure they know what to say next. 'I can imagine your voice travelling through the air.'

'It would have been a waste. My ma was right. God rest her.'

Our mothers. That's another thing Francis and I have in common.

'She would've liked you,' he says.

I knew Mrs Westaway to look at but I don't think I ever said two words to her and I certainly don't think she would have liked me. Everyone said she was the grumpiest woman east of Punt Road. Everyone said hers was the smallest funeral that St Ignatius had ever seen. That wasn't because of her manner though. That was on account of Connie.

'I'm sure I would have liked her too.'

He raises his eyebrows, pulls at his fingers, cracking the knuckles first and then the joints. 'Your father, he's healthy enough. Sometimes we do old people a disservice by mollycoddling them.'

'He's not so well as he used to be.'

'He'd probably do better on his own. You could still do his washing and ironing and shopping and take him round his tea.'

I nod but I don't have the foggiest what he means. Take him round his tea? From where? And of course I'd do his washing and ironing. What else would I do with my day? I'll always look after my dad. Not every man would've kept a child, especially a girl, when his wife died giving birth to her.

Francis stands in front of me. I tilt my neck to look up at him.

'Got ya something.'

He hands me a small red velvet pouch with a tiny gold drawstring. It takes me a moment to understand what he's said.

'Go on, then. Open it.'

The drawstring is tight but I tease it open and empty the pouch onto my palm. It is a pendant. A purple jewel a good inch long, set in gold, hanging on a chain. The setting is heavy, the chain is fine and warm-coloured. He can't be giving me this. Something like this could never belong to me.

'Don't you like it?'

'It's the loveliest thing I've ever seen.' I look down at it, sparkling in my palm. 'Francis. I can't accept it.'

'Why not? What's wrong with it?'

'Not a blessed thing. But it must be worth a fortune.'

'True.' He grins. 'Guess what it cost me. Guess.'

I can't imagine. It could be worth fifty pounds. More. Where would Francis get that kind of money? I shake my head.

'It cost me nothing. Can you believe it? Not a bean.' He's excited as a child, hugging himself, rocking on his heels.

He goes on to tell me a long story about how he used

to help old people in their yards when he was a boy, about the importance of respecting your elders, about a little hard work never hurting anyone. He called it his charitable works, he says, and he'd come home dirty and scratched from weeding and pruning, then be up half the night finishing his homework with Kip grumbling and growling about the light keeping him awake.

The pendant was a present from one of his old ladies. She was that grateful. *I didn't want to take it, of course.* She pressed it upon him. *Please, Francis. You've been like a son to me.* He's kept it all these years, hidden away, waiting for the right girl.

'And I thought to myself yesterday: the time has come. I bet Annabel Crouch would like that necklace,' he says.

The kind of boy he was. The kind of man he is. You could drive a truck between him and his and me and mine.

'You should've given it to your ma.'

He laughs like I've made a joke. 'It's from Europe, the old lady said. Italy maybe. She got it off a duke or a prince or something. I'm pretty sure. Maybe a count. What are you waiting for?'

I loop it around my neck. The clasp is so delicate that for a moment I'm scared of my clumsy fingers but then it's done. I can feel it, cool and smooth, resting at the base of my throat. From Italy, from a duke.

'That looks fine,' Francis says. 'I can't wait to show everybody.'

On the walk to the tram I feel like a different girl. I ask Francis to slow down and he does. I almost ask him to hold my hand. Inside the ballroom, there's a crush and a half. It's the biggest room I've ever seen, arches and balconies along the side. The band is playing and a few couples are dancing. Some men are standing down one end, girls at the other. Francis heads off to see his friends, most of them in the law too, all with big futures. I watch as a man hands him a silver flask from a pocket in his jacket. Francis tilts it high and drinks in one gulp, just like Dad.

Over against the wall sit Millie Mathers and Jos McCarthy. They look at me and speak to each other behind their hands. We were never what you'd call firm friends: every girl in Richmond knows every other to some degree, and for a time Jos worked in the munitions factory with me. She was in the office, of course, not on the floor.

I hold the pendant in my hand. Millie and Jos stand: they're coming over. They say hello, smile with tight mouths.

'Where have you been hiding yourself?' Jos says. 'My mother asked after you the other day. You should drop in for tea.'

I can't find the words to answer. I don't know the polite way to say, *Thank you. That's very kind. I'd love to come to your house but I must decline because there's no way I can ever return the invitation.*

'I like your frock, Annabel,' says Millie. 'It's sweet.'

'Every time you wear it, I like it all the more,' says Jos.

Millie and Jos work at George's, in ladies' wear. They have their own money and their own lives. I'd like to compliment their dresses, but I don't know what to say. I don't know how to describe the fabric or the trimmings. I can't find words for the colours: one is sombre green and the other reddy-pink, colours that must have their own names. They are dresses for drinking sherry in, not pouring beer.

'My, Annabel,' Jos says. 'Where did you get that pendant? It's beautiful.'

She means it. They are both staring hard and Jos leans forward and touches my chest when she picks it up, holds it, feels its weight. I tell them it is a gift from Francis. Millie and Jos look at each other.

'Oh,' says Jos. She drops the pendant like it's burned her.

'Oh indeed,' says Millie.

'You two aren't engaged, are you?' says Jos. 'We would have heard.'

'No. We're not engaged.'

They look at each other again. 'Funny,' says Millie. 'Francis giving you a pendant first.' She licks her lips. 'Not a ring.'

'Perhaps you shouldn't let that pendant become common knowledge, Annabel, dear,' says Jos. 'You don't want to give people the wrong impression.'

'I don't know what you mean.'

Millie smiles. 'You're such an innocent. It's charming.'

'You wouldn't want people to think it was a gift of gratitude from a man to whom you are not engaged,' says Jos.

More couples are moving on to the floor. The dancing is awkward at first, then faster and smoother. Jos spies someone across the room. She waves her arm as if she's drowning.

'Mac!' she calls out, and waves again, and he comes down

160

our end. It's her brother. I haven't seen Mac for years; he looks different in his army uniform and he's grown tall. He's the only boy down our end in a sea of girls; everyone stares and some of the women around us move back as if he might have something catching. Jos kisses him on the cheek and so does Millie.

'You remember Annabel Crouch?' she says.

He says he does and *how do you do* and shakes my hand. When he smiles, I can see the boy I knew.

'Mac's been over in Japan, getting the Nips sorted out,' says Jos.

'You look just the same, Annabel,' says Mac. 'Care to dance?'

I say I'd love to.

'Well,' says Jos. Millie's lips disappear entirely.

———————+———————

'Never realised quite how much of a soldier's life was spent dancing,' Mac says, above the music. 'Every leave, every night.'

He's right, though it's not the kind of dancing I remember. At school, before I left for munitions work, the nuns taught us what little they knew. They were Faithful Companions of Jesus and had never been to a proper dance in their lives. Stiff waltzing, white gloves, curtsies. They'd have a fit if they saw the jitterbug.

'My memory is: boys don't like dancing until they grow to men.'

He laughs. 'The year I did the merit certificate, my mother was dead keen on me learning to dance. I remember telling her I'd broken my leg and couldn't go. Footy training I could manage all right. The leg healed itself for that.'

'I'm thinking your mother was on to you.'

'I should have limped in a more, ah, convincing fashion. Old man gave me the strap for lying.' He opens and closes the palm of his hand like it still pains him. 'I was in strife every five minutes at home. Excellent training for the army.'

'And you don't hate dancing anymore?'

He smiles and goes to twirl me, then all at once he stops moving. Francis is standing beside us.

'Saint Francis,' says Mac. 'What's it been? Five years, six? What are you doing with yourself? Still riding that desk? Life must've been grand in a reserved occupation.'

'Annabel. We're leaving.'

'We were just dancing, Francis,' I say.

'I'm not sure the lady's quite ready to go,' says Mac. 'Tell you what. You have another drink and I'll give you a hoy when we're finished.'

'She came with me and she'll leave with me,' Francis says.

'Now, now, civilian,' says Mac. 'Don't go overwhelming me with gratitude.'

'Annabel.' Francis takes me by the arm but then Mac takes hold of Francis and he lets me go.

'I hate to argue, sunshine, but I will if I have to,' says Mac. 'And you know how that will go.'

I look from Francis's face to Mac's and back again. Everyone is waiting. Now someone comes up behind them both: a man, standing between Mac and Francis, a hand on each shoulder. For the first time since he's been back I notice how much he's filled out, broadened. Army rations and army work. The first thing that strikes me are those hands. They're nearly as big as Mac's and you can tell they're strong just by the look of them.

'Mac. You're back. Good to see you.'

Mac takes the outstretched hand and shakes it like he's drawing water from a pump. 'Kip Westaway. Him of the good timing: joins up when the war's as good as won.'

'Never fear mate, there was plenty of work to be done when I got there,' Kip says. 'Cleaning up after heroes like you.'

'How's the nose? Sorry, again.'

'Don't be. I've grown fond of it. It has a certain roguish charm, and it stops people mixing me up with my brother. And I would've messed yours up well and truly, if I could've landed a punch.'

They both laugh and throw pretend jabs at each other, ducking and weaving. Kip starts walking and steers Mac with one hand on his back, then he holds his arm out for me and says how nice it is to see me again, as if he's about to accompany me to a royal ball. I thread my arm through his and he leads us over to the side of the hall, on account of the dancers are nearly stepping on us. Francis follows, steam coming out his ears. Millie and Jos appear then and we spread out to become a circle of six.

Kip is full of questions about Mac's unit and what was it like in Japan and Mac says Japan was the real war, not just mopping up like Kip did in the Solomons and Kip says he was in Borneo too and that was no mop-up. He asks Mac whatever happened to Pike and Cray, who I don't remember because

I didn't know their sisters, I suppose. It turns out that Mac, Pike and Cray joined up at sixteen and their fathers signed the tricked-up paperwork with the idea it'd keep them out of worse trouble. Pike is an officer now and Cray is in a military prison for something or other.

'I'm so proud of my brother the war hero.' Jos squeezes Mac's arm. 'Kip. You took your time joining up, didn't you?'

Half of Melbourne knows why Kip took his time, of course. Jos knows. That's not why she said it. She just looks at him with a half smile on her face. For a minute no one says anything. I look at Mac. He clears his throat.

'Had to save some blokes for the end,' says Mac. 'And like Kip says, Borneo was no mop-up.'

'I couldn't go while Ma was alive.' Kip looks Jos square in the face when he says it. 'After Connie died, after the inquest and having it all in the newspapers. Having our business picked over by strangers. Most of the women in Richmond would cross the street when they saw Ma coming. Got so she wouldn't go out the front gate and then so she wouldn't get out of bed. I couldn't leave her.'

Jos has the decency to look at the ground and I'd like to turn away myself but I keep my eyes on Kip while he speaks. Francis is turning pink. I can't believe Kip talked about the inquest and everything out loud like that, just plain as you please. It's not the sort of thing you talk about in mixed company. The rest of Richmond whispered about it over fences and gossiped on street corners. It put the fear of God into all of us. For a while, anyway.

Mac coughed again. 'You still live next to the Hustings?'

Mac says. 'Jack Husting, what happened to him again?'

'North Africa,' says Kip.

So we all stand there amid the music and the bustle, still as statues, and we say nothing. Each of us is thinking about someone we'll never see again. That's what war means. It should be all over now and here we are at a dance but there are holes in the crowd. People missing who should be dancing and talking and living and breathing. I imagine for a moment the hall is filled with extra swaying couples. I can almost see them: young men in uniform and women in Saturday-night frocks. They look just like real people except when the light hits at a certain angle, it shines right through them.

'Annabel?' says Jos. 'Isn't it?'

I blink, and the dancing couples disappear and I'm back among the living and I'm glad that I'm here at a dance with Francis with so much to be thankful for that I could hug everyone.

'I said that's a beautiful pendant you gave Annabel,' says Jos to Francis.

Francis beams. Kip whistles and looks at Francis with his forehead all furrowed. 'Bloody hell. Where'd you get something like that?'

Francis doesn't speak. He's embarrassed, I can tell. Francis always pretends to be big and tough as if he doesn't care what anyone else thinks. But he does care. He's soft on the inside, I know it. He shouldn't be shy. It was helping other people that got him that pendant.

'Well?' says Kip.

Francis still doesn't answer, so I tell them. About the old

lady and the garden and how she was so grateful and gave him the pendant.

'Annabel,' says Francis. 'Shut it.'

'You shouldn't be embarrassed,' I say. 'Francis calls it his charitable works.'

'No, no.' Francis laughs and pats me on the arm. 'I never. I bought it from a jeweller in Collins Street. It was a little story I told her. She'd fall for anything. I was kidding.'

Everyone looks at me, then back to Francis. I can feel my cheeks burn. Millie starts to giggle.

'You made it up?' I say. 'There was no little old lady?'

'Well, well, Saint Francis. Haven't you got an active imagination?' says Mac. 'That's quite an interesting story. It seems to me I've heard something similar before, something from when we were boys. Because we were so close as boys, you and me and Pike and Cray. Charitable works, was it?'

'Don't pay any attention to her,' Francis says. 'She doesn't know what she's talking about.'

'That's right. I've mixed it up. I wasn't listening properly. It was from a jeweller. That's what Francis said.' He is so respectable and so modest. He'd hate for everyone to know he does charity work on the side. I've said the wrong thing again.

'I remember our boyhood years well, Francis. What a kind and generous lad you must have been,' says Mac. 'Honest. Fair to your friends.'

'Of course,' I say.

'You work in the law now, don't you? Quite a career for someone with your sense of justice,' says Mac. 'You're at McReady's, I remember.'

'You seem well informed,' says Francis.

'Campbell McReady is a friend of my father's, as it happens,' says Mac. 'He owns the whole firm. He'd be your boss, wouldn't he?'

'I suppose so.'

'Yes. I suppose he would be. I haven't seen Mr McReady for years and years. I should drop around in the morning and pay him a visit.'

The dance is heating up now. The music seems louder and couples are flying around, faster and faster. Mac and Francis have their backs to the dance floor: it seems like there's a wall of flashing colour behind them. I feel dizzy watching. It's very hot. I'd like a ginger ale. One light blue streamer has fallen down: it's resting on Francis's shoulder.

'It's like a zoo in here,' says Francis. 'Come on, Annabel.'

Outside the air seems cool in comparison. I didn't want to go: Leggett's doesn't give passouts, everyone knows that. The music is distant now, and my night of dancing seems miles away. I can feel one of the darts at my waist beginning to split. The problem with wearing my mother's clothes is that my mother had a nicer figure and moved with more grace. So upright and elegant, like a princess. I should have known better. Mac and the others have stayed inside. Out here, it's just me and Francis. He's pacing up and down in front of the hall, running his fingers through his hair.

'I'm sorry,' I say.

167

'You just don't know when to shut up, do you Annabel? Blabbing my business all over town.'

'I didn't mean to say anything wrong.'

'Do you not understand how sensitive a reputation is? It's up to me to be respectable. I'm the eldest. It's my responsibility.'

'If it was a secret, you should have told me.'

'I shouldn't have to tell you every little thing,' he says. 'Can you not have a bit of decorum, for God's sake?'

I don't speak.

'I know you weren't at school for long, but surely the nuns taught you how to act like a lady instead of a fishwife. Regardless of how you live at home.'

The air is very still. I am very still.

Then I say, 'What? What did you say?'

He shakes his head. 'Forget it.'

'No.' I can feel a rush inside me, heat moving up my body, and my ears are buzzing. There's an energy in my hands and in my legs that makes me want to start running. Run fast and never stop. 'What did you mean by that?'

'Francis.'

I turn my head and Kip is standing on the stairs to the hall. I can barely make him out with the light behind him.

'They're playing slower music now, easier to dance to,' Kip says. 'And someone's put out the sponge cakes. Annabel might like some cake and they won't last long. Like locusts in there. Francis, come back inside. You can sweet-talk the lady at the booth. Tell her you stepped out for a moment, to get some air.'

'Why don't you mind your own business?'

'It's all right, Kip,' I say.

'I don't want Francis to say something he might regret.'

'Regret?' Francis spins to look at him. 'I won't be the one who has any regrets. I'm trying to bring her up in the world. You'd think I'd get a bit more gratitude, seeing how she lives with her father.'

'Francis,' says Kip. 'This is the drink talking.'

'What, does she think nobody knows? Everybody knows. All of Richmond knows.'

I take a breath that I wish could last forever, so I never have to exhale again but I hear a creak and feel the seam at my waist give a little more. I want to go home. I can walk from here: it's not that far. But there's one thing I have to do first. I reach behind my neck and undo the pendant.

'Here.' My throat seems bare. I hold it out. 'I don't want this anymore.'

'Francis, don't you dare take that back,' says Kip. 'Don't you dare.'

'I wouldn't keep it if he got down on bended knee.'

'You've already accepted it. It's already yours,' says Kip.

'Keep out of it.'

'Francis. You can't take a gift back like that. It's not right.'

Francis turns to me. 'To think I was going to ask your father tonight. What a lucky escape. There'll be another girl more than happy to get a necklace like this. Any one of those girls inside, right now.'

'Francis. You gave it to Annabel. It's hers,' Kip says.

'She doesn't want it. She said.'

Kip walks over and takes the pendant out of my hand.

He holds it up to his eyes: it's dark out here. I wonder he can make it out.

'I'll give you ten pounds for it,' he says.

Francis snorts.

'Twenty.'

'Where would you get twenty pounds? What sort of wages do they give you at that pathetic job?'

'I'll give you a pound a fortnight, from my pay.'

Francis shuts his eyes for a moment, then opens them. 'Twenty-five.'

Kip feels around in his pockets and pulls out a note and a handful of change. 'Here. One pound two and six. Down payment.' Then he walks over and stands in front of me. I'm shaking. From the cold, I think.

'I don't want it, really. Give it to some other girl.'

'Look, Annabel,' Kip says. 'There's no point Francis taking back what he said. We're all so close together around here. There's no way to keep secrets in these little houses.'

I can barely keep my head up at that. At heart, I always knew everyone talked about my father and me. Passing me on the street and smiling, thinking their horrible little thoughts. Kip takes my hands and holds them in his. I can feel my mind calm, my breathing steady. Other than dancing, it's the first time I can recall that I've touched the skin of a man who isn't my father.

'Annabel Crouch,' he says. 'I know you want to be the one who does the honourable thing. But I'm asking you to be generous. I'm asking you to let someone else be honourable for a change.'

The difference between generous and honourable isn't something I've thought about before, but I look at Kip's face and see that this is important. I nod. Kip walks around behind me and reaches around my neck. One of his hands touches my shoulder and the other brushes my throat. His skin is warm and dry and soon I feel the pendant again, the familiar weight, the way it smooths my skin.

'You're a bloody idiot, Kip,' says Francis. 'Always were, always will be.'

———————✦———————

Francis heads back into the ballroom. I watch him buy another ticket, with Kip's money. Kip and I walk along the quiet streets in the dark. It's late, so we take the train back to Richmond. We aren't touching, but it doesn't matter. The skin on my hand remembers. We don't say much. When we get home, I thank Kip for the pendant, and for bringing me home. He says that without a doubt Francis will be over first thing, to apologise. *People fight, Annabel. What matters is how they make up, how they say sorry. He had a few too many, that's all. Mark my words.* Francis might come around tomorrow, and he might not. It'll make no difference to me. I've already made up my mind.

I say goodnight and Dad is sitting where I left him, as if it's only been a few hours instead of a hundred years. Most Saturday nights, I wish he was awake. I imagine him reading or listening to the wireless and waiting up for me. I'd make us tea and we'd sit up and talk for ages about everything that happened. What the other girls were wearing, what the band was like. Tonight I'm glad he's out cold.

Normally, I do whatever needs to be done to move him to bed. I like him to meet the morning horizontal, between clean sheets. On a good day he'll have sobered sufficiently to make it under his own steam with just a little prodding, and once he's in bed he won't wake until the early hours for his nightcap from the little bottle that he keeps buried under his singlets. Some kind of spirit or else port or sometimes sherry. Who does he think washes his singlets, irons them and folds them and puts them away? Yet every night he pretends I don't know about the bottle and I do the same.

'Dad.'

I touch his shoulder and without a word he's up and teetering towards the back door where he fumbles with the lock, then he stands just inside and relieves himself, out into the yard. I hear it, impossibly loud and long, and it sounds like he hasn't cleared the cement which means I'll have to wash down the stinking stain in the morning. I fetch two glasses of water from the kitchen and leave the one for drinking within reach of his bed. It'll be untouched when I clean tomorrow. He comes back in, fly buttons undone, trousers half off, reeking; he sits on the bed, eyes closed.

I kneel and lift his feet one by one to rest on my bent knee, untie his shoes and take them off, take off his socks. His limbs are limp and heavy, he does nothing to help me. I fold his arms out of his shirt, haul him to his feet to pull down his trousers, then sit him back down again. I hang up his pants and his belt. I hold my hand flat and he takes out his teeth

172

and drops them into my palm: warm and sticky, shiny pink and white. I put them in the spare glass on his bedside table and wipe my wet hand on the sheet, then pull it back, and he climbs inside. I kiss his forehead and turn to leave.

At the door, I stop. I can't forget what he said earlier tonight. I shouldn't disturb him. There's a risk he'll wake up properly, that he'll be angry, that he'll fight with the walls or the furniture or me. But I'll never sleep without knowing.

I walk back to the bed and kneel beside it. I can see the web of red veins around the sides of his nose. His eyelids droop into heavy folds. I can hear his breathing pause, like he's filled his lungs for the last time. He is killing himself, I know that. I won't have him for very much longer. The time will come when I'd give anything to put him to bed one more time.

'Dad.' I shake his shoulder. 'Dad. Wake up.'

He startles, his eyes and mouth bolt open in alarm and he clutches the sheet around him, a frightened boy wakened from a bad dream. I'm sorry I've disturbed him now. I should climb in bed beside him and sing him a lullaby, but I don't. I need him to answer.

'Hmmm? Wha'?'

'Kip Westaway. Francis's brother. Why don't you like him?'

He snorts the silly-Annabel snort and rolls over in the bed, turns his back. I hear him mumble. He speaks very softly.

'Take you away from me,' he says.

CHAPTER SEVEN

Jean

IF I'M NOT out the door by twenty to seven and on the tram I won't be in the kitchen by half seven and the missus insists upon punctuality and all the silver needs doing for the war widow dinner tomorrow night.

'Ma. Aren't you having any breakfast?' Kip is still in his pyjamas. This morning there isn't anywhere he is supposed to be. He's eyeing the last slice of bread. Boys that age, hollow in the middle.

'Couldn't fit a thing in,' I tell him.

'Ma could I have a ha'penny for a bun?' says Francis.

'Tomorrow.'

By rights it should be Connie's job to do the breakfast and I've already spent ten minutes I do not have looking for that girl. She's not in the kitchen. I look in the bedroom: she's not there either. I open the front door for a bit of breeze: just the usual workers dawdling past, rubbish blowing along with the wind, dust and soot and the smell from the tannery that blows up the hill. The rising tide of the world I spend every last breath keeping out of this house.

'Ma. Maybe I should go in next door,' says Kip.

'Go over later and look after the horse. Most boys'd be happy for a day off.'

How do you keep a civil tongue in this damn heat? And my head, it's cruel. I take the damp hanky out of my sleeve and wipe my neck with it. The pain comes from the bones above my eyes, pressing in and down. Kip plonks himself down right in the hall, panting like some animal.

'We have chairs for that,' I say. 'Your sister. Seen her?'

He drags himself to his feet like the world's against him and leans in the doorway to the bedroom. He shakes his head. 'Maybe there's something I can do. Make myself useful.'

That's the last thing the Hustings'll need, my youngest bobbing up, trying to make himself useful. I know full well what it's like in there: curtains drawn to make sure the day hasn't started and they'll be hoping it never does. No wireless playing, no one speaking. Ache in her stomach like a kick from a horse, wondering why they let him go, why they didn't bolt the door to his room while he was sleeping. Mr Husting will be wishing he could have yesterday over and over again, for ever. They'll be holding that telegram until it crinkles in their hands. She won't be so high and mighty today.

At least with Tom I had a body to bury.

'He used to help me brush Charlie, some days,' says Kip.

'Good of him,' I say.

'At the railway station, at the last minute. It seems like a couple of days ago. Doesn't seem nearly four months.'

'Time flies.'

'I think he changed his mind. I think he didn't want to go after all.'

'Too late by then, wasn't it.'

Kip has that set on his face that reminds me of his father, that wistful look. I'd never confess it to another living soul but some days I can't bear the sight of that boy. It's a judgment on me. He's Tom when he stirs his tea, clinking the spoon on the cup. Clink, clink. Tom when he tilts his chair to balance on the back legs. He'd snap one or the other if he fell: his back or the chair's, and who'd have to look after him then? Mugsy me. Those moments, when he reminds me of Tom, I have to leave the room. The fury rises up my legs and up my body like a scream and it's all I can do to not let it out. I go to the laundry and splash my face with cold water and count to fifty. Sometimes I'd like to slap him. My own boy, for the way he stirs his tea. Tom. I ask you. Falling off a tram. Sometimes I dream Kip is Tom come back to life and I let him have it good and proper for dying on me like that.

'Libya. That's in the desert. Must be a lonely place,' he says. 'I hope he had a good horse. I hope he didn't die alone.'

'We all die alone,' I say. 'No need to make a song and dance about it.'

Francis is flicking through his school books, showing

no signs of moving. 'Do you know where she is?' I say. He shrugs.

This is not how I imagined it to be. Children. Mothering. As a girl I had plenty of suitors but none like Tom. Best behaviour in front of my father, children brought up in the church all right by him. I saw myself in a rocking chair with a plaid rug around my shoulders and a wee one sleeping in my arms and another sitting quiet on the floor beside me. Embroidering, maybe. We'd have a piano. Tom would have a respectable job in an office and I'd have a girl to do the heavy work and he'd come home and smoke his pipe and read his paper in front of the fire. I saw myself brushing the babies' hair, watching them sleep on our big bed curled like kittens, breathing each other's sweet baby breath.

Then, just so: Tom won the treble only two weeks before the wedding. I remember the look on his face when he showed me, a fat roll of paper, more than I'd ever expected to see at once. Straight off he put down a cash deposit on this house and never laid another bet. Small and run down, yes, but half-way up the hill. Away from the slums. Funniest thing was: Tom never had any religion and ever since our wedding day, it was me that went over to his side. Oh, I kneel and speak the words, make the children go, even take the sacrament but fact is the Lord fell away from my life the moment Tom slid that ring onto my finger.

I am about to give up looking for that madam. Nothing will induce me to yell out for her like a fishwife. But then I spy her from the kitchen window. She's in the backyard of all places, under that awful tree, the one that'd be felled, uprooted, chopped up and burnt by now if I still had a husband to do it. Those berries leave stains that are a bugger to get out. It's hotter inside than out and she's sitting on the ground, hands on her stomach. Lord, don't let her be ill. No sense trying the boss's patience. Doesn't know how lucky she is, with a boss like Mr Ward. She should be on time, not give him any reason to complain. Sitting under trees can wait until she's married.

I call out 'Connie' but she doesn't look up. She's ignoring me. Right. She'll wish she'd come when she was called soon enough.

'What time do you call this?' I say. When I'm standing right there she raises her head and she's white as powder. Her clothes are crushed and crumpled and then I see they're yesterday's. There's no need for that: she's got a perfectly good nightgown and two blouses, one to wear and one to rinse out. I don't go peeking over her side of the room. That's why the wardrobe's in the middle, for a bit of privacy.

'Connie. Did you not go to bed last night?'

She's looking next door across the lane. The curtains are still drawn. The shop will stay closed today. Someone should write out a sign: shut due to family bereavement. Make sure they don't have customers knocking on the door all day. The priest, or minister or whatever they call them, he might be there already but neighbours and friends will give them until noon before they come, cakes in their hands. I know.

'Next door all this time,' she says. 'Just across the lane. One day we won't even remember what he looked like, not without reminding.'

179

'Young men die in war. It's a sad fact.'

My headache has moved: now it's a band like an overly tight hat. It feels like my skull doesn't belong on the top of my head and if I relaxed it'd fall right off. My neck is stiff, my back aches too, right down the bones in the middle and at the bottom of my spine, a dragging. I'm too old to work like a blackfella. Connie needs to get up, now.

'I saw the telegram boy on my way home yesterday.' Her eyes are rimmed red. I wonder if she's slept at all. 'I saw him ride ahead of me up Lennox Street and slow down to read the numbers. I saw him get off his bike and lean it against the fence.'

I didn't see the boy arrive, but Connie's not the only one who knew a telegram had come. I'm used to this row of little weatherboard houses making all kinds of noises in strange weather: the boards moaning and sighing, the gutters creaking, the whole lot of them shifting together in the heat and the cold. Last night was stinking and the street was full of a different kind of noise altogether. It was Ada Husting, keening well into the small hours. It's not a wonder Connie couldn't sleep.

I try to get her up again but she doesn't move. I tell her there's nothing wrong with her.

Then she looks me in the eye. 'Ma. There's a baby.'

'What do you mean, there's a baby? Here? In the backyard?'

I look at her, in her crushed and dirty clothes and no slippers, at her sick face and her lank hair, at her hands clasped around her belly. How thin she's got. How blind I've been.

180

Oh, she is a clever thing. A wonderful clever girl. I lean down and haul to her to feet and I hug her. She's surprised because we don't go in for that kind of thing: as my mother used to say, *there's a word for women who can't stop touching each other and it's not a very nice one.* But I can't help it. She's skin and bone in my arms. A good spew cleans out the body. A healthy pregnancy, a healthy baby. 'Connie. Mrs Ward, I should say. Mrs Constance Ward. Doesn't that sound respectable?'

'Ma.'

They'll have to get a wriggle on. Can't have her showing. Still, at his age, a widower already, no one expects a long engagement. 'We can have a wedding ready to go in six weeks. Eight at the outside.'

'Ma, please.'

I can have the room next to the baby. In the Hawthorn house. Francis and Kip can share a room and she'll need a nursery. How many bedrooms are there? More than five, I suppose. I can direct the domestics. There'd be more than one, I'd say, and I know better than anyone the kind of tricks girls like that get up to. Connie won't have to worry about a thing. 'Hawthorn's further from St Kevin's but that's neither here nor there. And Kip! Maybe Mr Ward can get him a job at the *Argus.*'

'Ma.'

I know. Kip can take Connie's job. That's a good idea. He talks about nothing but photographs these days. Connie won't be working, not after the wedding. Hawthorn wives don't work and besides, she'll have this one to look after, and Mr Ward's two. And likely more. I hope this one's a girl. Makes sense to have the girl first so she can be a little mother to the next one, the boy.

'Ma. Mr Ward had nothing to do with it.'

'You can't get in the family way by yourself, my girl. A man is necessary at some point.'

'It wasn't him.'

For a moment, my heart stops. I'd give the life of my son for her not to keep talking. I'd go back to the Church, back to confession. Drop to my knees, beg the Virgin right now to intercede for me. I'd even stop praying for Tom to come back.

'You can't have. You wouldn't be so stupid.'

She doesn't say anything. Her hands go back to her stomach and she leans against the tree. I fight my arms down to my side and even so I can almost see the red welt of my palm on her cheek and the thought of it gives me comfort. I brush off my black dress. Look anywhere but at her.

'Well, he'll be marrying you, whoever he is. No two ways, we're respectable people.'

'No.' She laughs in a cold way. 'No, he won't.'

This is the job of a father. 'Don't you mind about that. There's ways and means. I'll talk to him myself. And if he doesn't come around, I'll speak to the parents and his parish priest. There's weight that can be applied.'

'You'll bring his parents into this?'

I nod. We're a decent family. We're halfway up the hill. 'Anyone who takes advantage of a girl deserves the shame of it.'

'Can't you leave his parents be?'

'No. This boy. What's his name?'

She doesn't answer. I ask her again. She shakes her head.

'I won't have everyone knowing,' she says at last. 'Gossiping, judging him.'

Of course he'll be judged, that's the point. Where does she think we live, Toorak? Somewhere with big houses and wide streets and people who don't even know their neighbours' names, far less their business? You can't keep secrets around here.

'If it comes to that, I'll go away. There are places I can go, aren't there?' she says. 'To have it.'

I'm glad her father is dead and I'm furious with him, so mad I could kick his headstone. How I hate that man, dying and leaving me all alone to look after everyone. I look at her and I can see her face is set. She always was willful, since she was little. I can see her blinking. She's thinking as far ahead as she can manage and it's not far.

'There are places like that. The Good Shepherd sisters in Abbotsford. Others in the country. And do you know how they're common knowledge? Because I can tell you every girl in Richmond who's been sent.' Gone to visit relatives in Brisbane, bad case of measles, God knows the rubbish people come up with. Reappear eight months later, bursting into tears if anyone looks sideways, a bust three times bigger and leaking down their front if they see a little one. Can't get a decent boy to step out with them. Life ruined. Nobody fooled for one moment.

'I'm having it. I don't care.'

Having it, and then handing it over like a stray cat to the nuns. Women who've sworn that motherhood means nothing. Does she not see what that'd do to a girl? You'd never recover.

183

Susan McCoy told me they let her daughter hold it for ten minutes and she's never seen it since. She doesn't care, Connie says. Oh Mother of God, grant me patience. My daughter squats there under the tree and from the look on her face she's going to be sick. That settles it: she's not too far along. Six weeks, no more. There's still time.

'I can't decide right away,' she says. 'We'll talk tomorrow.'

'If it's to be done, it's best done now.'

'Done away with, you mean.'

'By the time you get to my age you'll know some rules belong to Jesus and other rules belong to men who want to keep others in their place,' I say.

She looks at me. 'I won't.'

In our family we're not ones for big speeches, but standing there under that tree while the morning ticks away I talk as much as I ever have in one stretch. I tell her about shame and the way it's always the women who wear it. I spare her nothing. I say *loose woman* and *no morals* and I say *bastard* and I say *slut*. It pains me to hear these words in my own voice and I tell her to imagine how much worse they'll sound when filthy urchins are yelling them at her on street corners. I grit my teeth. When the children were little and there was TB around I made them take cod liver oil off a spoon even when they begged me not to. Medicine leaves a bad taste but it makes you better.

She never weeps. Not one tear. She won't relent.

But I'm not done yet. I know how to make her see sense. The boys. It's not enough that the world knows the state their father was in when he died, what about their own sister?

184

Does she want Kip to be ashamed of her too? Is that the burden she wants that boy to bear? I tell her how her father did everything to pull us halfway up the hill for the sake of his children and that she'll be the one dragging us down to the bottom of it.

When I talk about the boys she raises her head and I know I've reached her. It's Kip, especially. She'd do anything for him. She twists and turns her skirt between her fingers. Then she nods and I sag with relief.

I was twenty hours in labour with Connie. She was so still when she came out, like wax. But I knew she was a girl. And when the midwife handed me Francis, so tiny, almost purple, coated in grease—then she said there was one more coming and I thought she was having a lend of me when out popped Kip, squirming and mewing. A husband and three littlies. The best days of my life. The reason women are put on earth. There's still hope for her, to have a husband and children the right way, keeping them and not giving them up.

'Right,' I say. 'Get inside. Neither one of us will be going to work today.'

Mothers need to know that butter goes on a burn and spider webs on a cut, clove oil for a toothache, cakes and tea for bereavement. And for things like this, for girls like Connie and saving her future, there is a respectable woman who runs a business in Victoria Street.

'Aren't you going to work, Ma?' says Francis.

They're still sitting at the kitchen table like two Lord Mucks. I've changed out of my uniform. Connie is in our room sitting on her bed, looking like even getting into clean clothes is too much for her.

'Kip. Did you ever notice your sister stepping out with a boy?'

He looks up like I've dropped something. 'Stepping out? A boy?'

'Got fairy floss in your ears? Yes. A boy.'

'A man's sister,' says Francis. 'I'd fix anyone who tried.'

'Wasn't asking you. Well?'

'No,' he says, slow and careful.

'You'd tell me if you knew anything.'

'Course I would.' He blinks more times than is normal.

'Is Connie all right?' says Francis.

'She's crook. I'm going to stay home and look after her.'

'It's not fair,' says Francis. 'Kip gets to stay home, you and Connie get to stay home. Why do I have to go to school? It's holidays.'

'You're the one that asked for extra. Good of the brothers to let you.'

'When I'm a rich lawyer I'll have buns for breakfast every day. I won't ever eat bread again.'

Kip jumps up from the table. 'I'm getting dressed,' he says. 'I'm going to feed Charlie.' He just about runs to the bedroom.

'What's the matter with him?' says Francis.

'Your brother has a soft heart.'

I open the second drawer and take out a notepad and

186

pencil, write a shopping list and two notes, thinking about every word, in my neatest hand. I call Kip back and give him instructions after he's seen to the horse: first, go to the big house and drop off the note explaining. There's a good chance I'll keep that job. With more and more women going to the factories good housemaids are hard to find.

Then, the second note to Mr Ward at the *Argus*. Connie's got the flu. Bad. It's best she stays home for the week.

Then I tell him to drop by his father's grave and give it a clean up and then as he's in the city he can go to the Vic Market and get some necks and giblets so I can make soup for Connie. And Francis: he can take his cricket boots so he can go to practice straight after school. I tell them Connie will need her peace and quiet.

'That'll take all day,' Kip says. 'Maybe if Connie's sick Mr Ward'll let me go with the photographers today. He's always saying to come in. He says they'd be glad to have the help.'

I think of Connie sitting under that tree. The shame that comes from behaving in ways you oughtn't. Kip gave up his chance. I shake my head.

———✦———

When I've got rid of the boys I go upstairs. Connie is curled in a ball under the covers, in this heat. I get her up, get her dressed. She does as she's told for a change, doesn't ask any questions. Before we leave, I take the bundle of notes from under my mattress. For a moment, as I hold it in my hand, I almost change my mind. It's all we have.

187

On a normal day we'd walk down the Vaucluse to Church Street but today we take three trams: down Swan, up Church and back up Victoria. On the last tram, the lady conductor takes one look and barks at a working man to give up his seat. Connie doesn't argue, sinks into it like a puppet with its strings cut. In Victoria Street, I have one arm around her waist. She's leaning on me, making no effort. Reluctant, but without the strength to walk away.

I know what she's thinking. She's thinking it's all too hard, that it'd be easier for all concerned if she took the tram the other way up to the Church Street bridge and did a swan dive into the Yarra. It seems every other week they drag that filthy drain and find some poor soul stuck on the bottom, snagged on some piece of rubbish. Maybe they're better off without their troubles and maybe they aren't, but one thing's for sure: it's a coward's way out, else I'd have done it myself by now. Three children and working like a slave to feed them. Not what I would have chosen either.

When we stop in front of the shop, Connie looks up. She's surprised. I know what she was expecting: a stinking back alley littered with rotten vegetables and horse manure. A Chinaman with filthy nails and sour breath. As if I'd do that to my little girl. We're out the front of an elegant dressmaker's set demurely between a tea shop and a gentlemen's outfitters. Sparkling window, gold lettering on the glass, the inside clean and crisp, mannequins in the latest fashions and bolts of silk along one wall. I think how nice it'd be to have silk in one of those shades for Connie's glory box, but you can only spend money once.

I push the door and the little bell tinkles. The shop is divided in half by a velvet curtain and there's a girl sitting at an elegant desk. The desk has skinny curved legs that look highfaluting in a place like this but back where I grew up would remind everyone of rickets. The girl is wearing a suit in a minted tweed. She nods her head in a serious way and looks down her long nose. She asks if she can help us.

'We're here to see Mrs Ottley.'

Her mouth says, 'Certainly madam,' while her eyes say *shouldn't you be using the servants' entrance?* 'In the meantime, would madam like to see some pattern books? Is it for a special occasion? For you, or the young lady?'

'My daughter, Constance. And it's a personal matter.'

She gives me a look and I know she understands. 'This way then,' she says, with a flick of her head and a voice sliding away from Hawthorn and closer to Richmond. I sit Connie down in one of the flimsy French chairs against the wall. She doesn't ask how I knew where to bring her. She hardly seems to know or care where we are or what it is I'm doing to save her. The girl lifts the curtain and I follow her through to the back of the shop.

'Wait here,' the girl says, and there's no madam anymore, and the space where that madam used to be is like a kick in the guts. It strikes me that this is why I'm doing this. It's so Connie has a chance of being a madam, for the rest of her life and the lives of her daughters and her daughters' daughters.

I stand in the back of the shop and wait. Nobody offers me a chair. Along one wall is a low bench with a row of working women all bent over sewing machines, feeding dresses and blouses and skirts through the wee feet, peering at the tiny stitches. Their broad legs pump the pedals, their quick hands change the direction of the fabric, loop the thread over and under to start a new seam. Every so often one stands, picks up a tiny pair of scissors and snips off the thread, then chooses a new reel of cotton from a vast rainbow on the other wall, walks back to her place and runs the end of the cotton between her lips and rethreads the machine. It'd be a good job, this, better than mine. Sitting down all the blessed day, easier on the joints. Though I probably wouldn't have the eyes for it these days. The women don't talk or even look up. It's as if I'm not here.

In a corner of the room, an old woman wearing a floral apron sits hunched on a stool darning something heavy, perhaps denim. In the broad shaft of light that comes through the windows high on the back wall I can see the needle flashing as she works. Sometimes the cloth is too thick and the needle doesn't want to go all the way through so she pushes the eye end against the pad of her thumb and forces the point of it through the fabric like a lance. All the while the expression on her face does not change. She doesn't feel a thing. Her thumb must be one solid lump of callous.

'Mrs Westaway,' says Mrs Ottley. She's come up behind me unnoticed and when I turn, her arms are crossed over her bosom like she's the Queen deigning to walk among us. Her hair is in a French bun to match the severe tailoring. She has wee spectacles on the tip of her nose and a belt around her waist holding a pincushion filled with shiny silver pins all clustered together.

Mrs Ottley is the picture of good deportment and her own best advertisement: she has a discreet pocket sewn into the waistband of her skirts to hold her business cards. Her hands, though, are rough and flakey with great knobby knuckles that stand out a good half inch. I'd reckon she hasn't always been such a lady.

'Mrs Westaway.' Her gaze goes straight to my belly. 'It's been some years since you've needed our assistance.'

'And as my husband hasn't miraculously come back to life, I have no need for it now.' I pull back my shoulders. As if she has the right to condescend to me. 'Mrs Ottley' indeed. I've lived in Richmond my whole life and I've never heard of a Mr Ottley. 'My daughter, however, is waiting in your front room.'

'How far?' The genteel dressmaker is gone now; the eyes are sharp as one of her needles.

'A few weeks, maybe. Can't be long. She's sick as can be.'

'Bring her through to the last fitting room on the right. And it's twenty-five pounds these days, Mrs Westaway.' She gives me a smile. 'War-time expenses.'

I close my eyes for a moment. That's all of it. Nothing in reserve for if I get sick or to pay for Connie's wedding or if something happens to Kip and we don't get his wages from the Hustings. Some days I feel disaster lurking around this family the way the soot floats down from the factories over all of Richmond, respectable or not.

'Or seeing as you've been a good customer in the past, I could do two for forty-five,' she says. 'Fix up your daughter now, keep one up your sleeve for yourself. Whenever you might need it.'

'That won't be necessary.' I put out my hand to give her the roll of notes but she pulls back her palms as if touching it would affront her delicacy.

'No, no,' she says. 'Give it to Katie, at the desk.'

I do as she says and go to fetch Connie. It takes all my strength to get her on her feet. We walk through the curtain, past the sewing women. They do not give us the slightest glance. The last fitting room is bigger than the others, with a door instead of a curtain. Inside is a long bench and some metal instruments in a tray. In the corner is a bucket with a lid. There is a strong smell of carbolic, and something else. Camphor? There is one window high up, glazed with dirty louvres.

'Take your shoes off, Connie,' I say, and she does. I put them in the corner out of the way. They're good shoes. Wouldn't do to have them stepped on.

'Your stockings.'

I stand behind her while she takes them off and I fold them up and put them in my handbag to take home.

'Up on the bench now.' She wriggles up and sits there, facing forward, hands over her belly.

'Ma,' she says, as I lay her down. 'It's all I have of him.'

'You'll have others. Bend your knees, there's a good girl,' I say. 'Feet flat on the bench. And best take off your knickers. Don't want them ruined.'

She grips my hand like she'll pull it off at the wrist. I'd like to tell her there's nothing to be worried about. That half the married ladies of Richmond have lain on that little bench at one time or another, that it's just something to be got through.

Part of being a woman. Mrs Ottley hasn't built up a business like this by letting things go wrong. She must do two or three a day, no trouble, things how they are these days.

The door opens: it's the old woman who was darning the denim. She's replaced her floral apron with a leather one and she is carrying a bucket full of steaming water.

'Don't get settled,' she says to me. 'It's not the MCG. We got no room for spectators.'

'Ma, please.'

'Give her this,' she says, and she opens the little cupboard under the sink and pulls out a bottle of brown liquid that might be whisky, and a small glass. She pours some for Connie, a healthy inch and a half.

I take the glass and lift it to her lips. She looks at me and I'm struck again by the memory of giving her the cod liver oil, those big eyes trusting me to do right by her. Now, as then, she takes it without a murmur and only after she swallows does her face screw up with the bitterness of it and one hand goes to her throat, which must be burning and she coughs a little. She's not used to strong liquor. At least there's that to be thankful for.

'If you're scared of this little thing, how would you ever have had a baby?' I say.

'Babies are worse,' says the old woman. 'No comparison.'

My fingers are starting to hurt from her squeezing. I look down: our hands are white and so close together, for a moment I lose sight of which fingers are hers and which are mine. The skin is stretched tight over the knuckles and they're pale and smooth like raw bone and still she won't let go. On the back of her hand, I can see the web of blue veins like tiny rivers. There's nothing for it. I can't stand here all day. I use my other hand to peel off her clinging grip.

———————✦———————

There's no point hanging around at Mrs Ottley's, nicking back every two minutes to see how things are going, being ignored by those sewing women, pacing uselessly like a man outside a maternity ward. Bedside manner, like the doctors do it. Crueller, kinder. Sometimes these things take hours to pass so I pop home to do the housework: Connie'll be off her feet for a few days at least and she'll rest easier if everything's done. I can't remember the last time I was in the house alone.

It's a luxury I'd long forgotten. I doubt I've had a minute to myself since I was pregnant with her. That first quickening, you never forget it. The first time you feel it, a cross between a squirming and a kicking, and you realise there's another whole body enclosed within yours, and it's made out of your very own flesh. While there's a child of yours alive in the world, you never really die. They're a part of your body living on without you. Connie kept me up at night and made me uncomfortable all day with her wriggling. I'd be walking to the shops and boof! A tiny wee knee in the kidney or a heel wedged between two of my ribs. She was my first to term so I thought it was normal. Now I know she was a restless child. The boys were both squeezed in there together and they were lazy as badgers.

Doing housework for yourself is different from doing

someone else's although it's the same work exactly. The same sweep of the broom, the same scrubbing of the laundry. There's a pleasure to it, when it's all your own. A sweetness. When I'm mopping the kitchen floor with the water from the washing I look out the window at the Hustings'; curtains still drawn as though there weren't a soul alive in there. Losing a son would be worse than a husband, I grant you. Husbands, you expect them to look out for themselves. And if they do something so stupid as to get themselves too drunk to hold on to a moving tram, with no consideration for the lives of their dependents, what could a wife be expected to do? They brought him home, the police that picked him up off the road. They said it was best he lie here though we had no room for it. In the end, the undertaker sent over some men with a pair of trestles and we took the door off the laundry and they set it up in the sitting room and washed his face and changed his clothes before we sent him on his way. If I had my time again, I wouldn't of let them lay him out here. I'd of made them take him away. He stank of rum and he'd wet himself. It was no way for the children to remember him.

At the Hustings', there's no body to lay out. Losing a child. The grief would only be the half of it. It's your job to look after them, to make sure things go in the natural order: that's you first, them second. I can see the upstairs windows. There's movement in the curtain then it settles back as it was. Perhaps it was the wind. Today will be the worst of it. To be in that house, alone, adrift, childless.

Tonight will be busy at our place. Connie will be resting, but all the neighbourhood women will visit to talk about

195

the telegram and what it said and how it happened exactly and where he was and how the Hustings were taking it. It's not gossip, exactly. It's keeping tabs, making sure everyone knows what's what before they knock on the door to pay their respects. I move away from the window and look at the clock. Time to get Connie.

———✦———

I thought she looked pale before. In the feeble light from Mrs Ottley's dirty louvres, she is white and light as a cloud. She's still on the bench and there's a pile of soiled linen in a corner. The shop is quiet and empty: all the sewing women have gone home. Mrs Ottley and Katie have gone home. Standing in the doorway is the old darning woman whose name I never thought to ask, who let me in when I knocked. She picks up Connie's shoes from the floor and forces them on her splayed feet, hooks her fingers along the heel to make them sit right. Connie offers no resistance or help.

'I gived her a belt and a towel. You'll need to change it.'

I nod.

'And no lifting anything heavy for a while.'

Connie's eyes are half open but she looks at me. She can see me.

'Ma. I want to go home.'

'Yes, yes. Come on then. I've changed your sheets and made the bed. It's all waiting.'

The old woman takes hold of the back of Connie's shoulders and sits her up. She swings Connie's legs around and takes one arm around her neck and I take the other and we get her to the front door. She props Connie against the window while she gets her bag and hat, and then turns off the lights. We all go out together. Connie's legs down the step one by one while the woman takes her weight.

'Sweet tea. If she's still bleeding by the weekend, a hot bath to bring on the rest of it. And no relations for a good two weeks.'

'The very idea,' I say.

Out on the street the old woman locks and bolts the door behind us. She adjusts her hat, nods at us, turns and walks the other way, her broad back winding down the street and crossing at the corner. That's the last I see of her.

It seems hotter than when the sun was straight above and the wind is swirling leaves and papers in circles down the street. It's the kind of night when young people catch a tram down to St Kilda and sleep on the beach. The paper tomorrow'll be filled with pictures of them, pillows and all. I need to get Connie home before the boys, have her tucked up in her own bed with a nasty dose of flu so they'll leave her alone and no nosy questions.

On the street, Connie's no help at all but somehow she's not as heavy as this morning. Passersby step around us, heads down, almost colliding with these women walking two abreast, shoulder to shoulder. Sometimes Connie goes over on her ankles and doesn't fall, she's that easy to carry. A tram comes along: we're on it and she slips her hand through the straps and stands suspended. She's woozy, as you'd expect.

There's hardly any passengers. The next two trams are easy as well. At our stop I almost lift her down the stairs, no trouble.

Nearly there now. We're in front of the London Tavern when she doubles up like she's been kicked in the guts. I can't keep hold of her, she bends over that fast and wriggles out of my grasp. I lean her against the wall to change my grip, lose hold of her altogether and she slides down until she's sitting on the ground.

'Connie.' It must be close to five. There's no one around now but it won't be long. 'We've got to get you up.'

No answer. I sit back on my haunches to think of the best way to move her and my knees ache like something's going to pop. Then I see a dark stain along the bottom of her dress and think: just my luck for her to choose a puddle to sit down in. I'll have to soak that as soon as we get home, maybe sponge it with some eucalyptus oil. She's nothing else to wear to work next week if her good dress is ruined.

I reach for the hem to move it out of the way and find the bluestone underneath is dry. The stain is creeping along the bottom of the dress and spreading upwards. I touch it with my hand and even before I bring my hand to my nose, I can smell it: rich and metallic. A rusty iron roof after rain, baking in the sun.

I move the dress and I see the thin spreading tide of blood as it seeps down between her legs. You'd expect blood but there's too much here to be right, I know that. I try to lift her again but I can't manage it. She's not light anymore. She's a dead weight in my red hands.

'Connie. You have to stay here while I get someone to help. Just don't move.'

She opens one eye and says, 'We're moving out west. He'll like that.'

'Just stay here a minute,' I say, and I straighten her against the wall and I wish I had my scarf or a coat so I could tuck her up like she was in bed. 'There'll be people down on Swan Street. I'll be back before you know it.'

'I'm sorry I didn't tell you earlier, Ma.'

'It doesn't matter now.'

'I was going to have it,' she says, clear as a bell, like she was sitting at the kitchen table and we were talking about what we had in the cupboard for the boys' tea. 'I decided. I wrote to him. He was going to come back to me and I'd be here and the baby'd be here and we'd both be waiting.'

'Sshh.'

'Ma, it's down the side in a biscuit tin. Him and me.'

'Wait one minute. I'm off to fetch someone. Someone to help.'

'It's all right, Ma,' she says. 'I won't go anywhere.'

When Connie was a wee baby, I used to leave her in the laundry tub sometimes, having her bath. She'd kick her fat legs and try to grab the water in her fingers. Every mother knows the dangers and I don't know how I trusted her to do as she was told. I'd never of done it with the boys but Connie, she was different. I'd tell her *I'm leaving for a bit* and *be good now* and *be on your best behaviour* and *sit up nicely in the water and don't drown*, and I'd hang the washing on the line or go out to check the letterbox and sure enough, she'd be right there where I left her, good as gold, still splashing away.

That's what I'm thinking about when, in that fading light in the empty street, I leave her alone for just a moment. No one can see us up this street, even if I yelled my lungs out. I'll walk as far as the corner, maybe fifty feet away, to find someone who could lift her by one arm while I took the other. To get her on her feet, home to her own bed. I tell her I'm leaving, and to be good until I get back. It's hot but I'm shaking and I run, then I look up and down Swan Street at the people rushing home, hats held down against the blustering wind. I'm only going to be gone for a minute. That's the only reason I leave her.

CHAPTER EIGHT

Alec

PICTURE THIS: Punt Road at twilight. Leaves blowing along the gutters, bumper shining against bumper, flattened light coating everything in its milky glow. Cars filled with people going home to the bosom of their loving families. The vermillion of glossy paintwork, the emerald of the trees around the oval. Above me the clouds are free, coasting, boasting to the earth of their fluffiness, drifting home with the traffic. Way overhead is a minuscule jet going somewhere better than here. Peace is far away.

Yet here I am. Away from home in a world of strangers. Alone. Forgotten.

I am sitting on the footpath between the pub and the brothel, leaning against a white picket fence. I make a square from my fingers and hold it up to frame a tree, the edge of a building, the train tracks on the bridge. A futile attempt at composition. I have no easel, no sketchbook. Not even my backpack. I left in such a hurry I brought nothing with me. Nothing except the shutter of my eyelids, the nubbed pencil of my memory.

If I had a mobile I could call the guys and find out where they are, but I, of course, do not have a mobile. Charlotte won't let me, because Charlotte lives in fear of brain-melting death rays and, more to the point, is intent on making me a leper. Lep. Per. For all intensive purposes, I already am. My foot might as well drop off right here in front of the Cricketers' Arms.

The guys are probably going out to have actual fun, something Charlotte has never heard of and wouldn't approve of if she had. Maybe they're at the movies. Or at Tim's playing Xbox in the garage. Tim, who has a mobile phone of his own that he doesn't even pay for. Tim, who has a mother who owns a car that she parks on the street especially to leave the garage free for him and his big brother; a garage that contains a ping-pong table under which he hides the beer his brother buys him.

Dude, Tim said, when I told him I couldn't go out tonight. *Bummer.*

When I left Rowena Parade this afternoon, Charlotte was all *don't you dare walk out on me Alec don't you dare.* She is ruining my life.

Charlotte, in contrast to Tim's mother who is cool, walks into my room like it's her own personal property. No knock, no *can I come in*, no nothing. She won't even let me have a lock on the door, not that a lock would keep Charlotte out. An iris scanner might do it. That would be wicked, actually. That would even stop Libby. Maybe I can install one myself; how hard can it be? Maybe they have them at Bunnings or Stewart's or one of those hardware behemoths.

I look at my watch, the symbolic shackle that marks me as the only person in the universe without a mobile phone— though if I did have one, she'd be on it the whole time telling me to come home and set the table for dinner.

Stanzi, on the other hand, would never call. Stanzi understands that I'm almost seventeen and practically a fully fledged adult. Soon I'll have my learner's, then in a couple of years, hello freedom. I'll be off like a shot, just watch me. It's not logical, the way Charlotte behaves. In two years I'll be making all my own decisions anyway: it's patiently obvious she should let me get some practice. I pass all my subjects and top the class in art. I'm not a cone head. No arrests for shoplifting. It's not like she's got anything to worry about.

The sun is going down and part of me wants to keep walking. Head down to Richmond Station and hop a train, see where it leads me, watch the landscape reveal itself. Mountains and rivers and deserts and oceans. This waiting for my life to start, it's driving me mental. I stand and begin walking up the hill. It's time to go home.

When I come through the front door, it's almost six. Libby is standing near the dining-room table, which is pulled into the middle of the room and extended full length. She's polishing knives and forks and spoons and placing them upright in chipped metal jugs that Charlotte found scouring op shops the length and breadth of Bridge Road because everything we own has to be secondhand so we can be marked as freaks in front of the whole neighbourhood. Also on the table is a pile of cloth napkins of different colours weighted down with a smooth rock. An actual rock, from near the Yarra at Abbotsford. Charlotte Westaway, eco-warrior.

'Muuuum,' yells Libby. 'He's baaaack.'

'World Sucking Champion 2006 strikes again,' I say. 'I can see why you're so popular with the boys.'

She turns a plum colour. 'You absolute prick,' she whispers, so Charlotte can't hear. 'I've been stuck here for hours.' She holds up her fingers in front of my face. 'I had to peel two tonnes of potatoes. Two. Tonnes. By. Myself. Look at my cuticles. Look at them.'

'Cry me a river, Justin friggin' Timberlake.' She's turning puce now. I can see the fires of rage burning behind her eyes. I wave my hand in front of my face. 'Is that smoke coming out of your ears? Libby? I've warned you about trying to think before. Quick someone, call triple zero, her neurons are melting.'

She gnashes her metal teeth. 'This is so unfair. I would *never* get away with that. It's just because you're a boy.'

What does she expect me to do? Crawl into the feeble position and beg forgiveness? I shrug. 'That's just the way the chromosome crumbles, Transformer-mouth.'

Libby gives me her *fuck off and die* look. I go upstairs to my room and lie on the bed and take out my sketch pad ready for the face of maternal fury which should appear at my door with digital precision. Yup. After exactly three minutes, the door opens.

'Come in,' I say.

'Don't you ever do that again,' Charlotte says. 'Run off while I'm in the middle of talking to you.'

'Yes, Charlotte.' *I shall stay here forever, waiting for your command, at your beckon call my queen.*

'And don't call me Charlotte.'

'Yes, *Mother.*'

'And why do you have to be so mean to your sister? She's fourteen years old. She looks up to you. And take your shoes off before you lie on the bed. That doona cover doesn't wash itself.'

I kick my Converses off and they thud on the floor. 'Anything to oblige, guv'nor. But I was back in time for roll call. Did the other inmates miss me?'

She shuts her eyes and then her lips start moving. Silent counting, her latest anger-management technique. Or, actually, Alec-management technique. I do a rough sketch in about eight seconds. I've seen that face a zillion times before. I can fill in the details later: the colours, the way the edges of her eyes and nostrils flare, the way her face looks like Stanzi's and mine and only a bit like Libby's, who has Ben's eyes. The ways we are all the same, the ways we are different. When she's finished counting she opens her eyes.

'Go downstairs and help your sister set the table. They'll be here in half an hour.'

'No thanks. I think I'll stay up here in my room and play with my Xbox. Oh. That's right. I don't *own* an Xbox. Never mind. I'll watch TV in my room instead. Oh, that's right. I'm not *allowed* a TV up here. Even when I offer to get a job and pay for it *myself*. On account of I live in *Nazi Germany*.'

'I'll make you a deal. When you're an adult, you can do whatever you want. You can play computer games twenty-four seven if you like. Shower once a year to celebrate Joss Whedon's birthday. Pee into a bottle.'

'Good. I might just do that. But the first thing I'll do, the second I turn eighteen, is get a tattoo. A big one. Right here.' I make a fist, roll up my sleeve and trace the outline on my tricep.

'Yes, that would be smart. Ten years ago you wanted a Dorothy the Dinosaur stuffed toy more than life itself. People change, Alec. A tattoo, that's for the rest of your life, you understand?'

You understand? Like I don't, like I'm an idiot. 'I'm not afraid of making decisions that affect the rest of my life.' Unlike her, the quintessential woman afraid of commitment. Ipso facto, two children, no boyfriend.

She turns and walks to the door. 'Stanzi,' she yells. 'Come and talk to your nephew before I stuff him in a cardboard box and mail him to the starving children in Africa.'

'You'll need a big box. He doubles in height on a weekly basis,' Stanzi yells back from downstairs. 'What are the starving children supposed to do with him?'

'Whatever they like,' Charlotte says. 'Target practice. Protein supplement. Scaring off wild animals. I'm not fussed.'

Starving Africans. Another epic bout of predictability from Charlotte Westaway, the last of the bleeding hearts. Case and point: when we were little she brought home lost kittens and baby birds that fell out of nests. She cries when she sees those swollen-stomach babies on the news.

On her way downstairs, Charlotte'll cross paths with Stanzi, who also comes when she's called. If she was in the middle of donating a kidney, she'd still come running. That's because both of them are terrified that Libby or me will suddenly think: *Wait a minute! I don't know how we didn't notice this before now, but...we don't have fathers!* I mean, I have a hairy old blues musician who lives on an avocado farm near Mullumbimby and sends me birthday cards at random times of the year, and Libby has some hot-shot Singaporean software designer who has this whole other family that she visits for two weeks in the Christmas holidays, but that's it. Charlotte and Stanzi fill every gap, answer every question. The perfect parental tag team. The smother mothers.

Charlotte will be going down slowly, at peace with the world (except me). I can hear Stanzi running up the stairs, two at a time, as if she doesn't burn enough kilojoules jogging around like a maniac all day. Why anyone would want to be a personal trainer is beyond me, especially when all her clients are depressed fat people, yet she's just busting to spend more energy running up the stairs whenever Charlotte yells. What Stanzi has is a fatal failure of the imagination. There is no other possible explanation for why she lives here.

Since the door is already open, Stanzi doesn't knock either. She doesn't look around my walls, which are covered in fluoro colours and tags and sweeping shapes left over from my graffiti phase. Pretty good ones actually but still, kind of lame. I need to repaint, if ever I have a minute to myself. Stanzi walks in and spreads herself across the bottom of the bed the way she did when I was little. She's already in her party clothes: a sequined black dress made from artificial fibres that requires drycleaning on a regular basis. I suspect she does this just to piss Charlotte off. One of the reasons I like her.

'What's up, kiddo?'

I groan. 'You mean apart from my mother bringing me up Amish?'

'Those black hats, though—so practical. As far as UV protection goes.' She stretches out on her back, arms and legs reaching to the walls. 'Hey, you know what would bring out your manly features? A chin beard. Here. Hold still.' She reaches down to the floor where my pastels are lying and picks up the black one. She wields it with what is intended to be a demonic cackle.

I roll away. She doesn't understand what I have to content with. 'Do I get a choice in this house? Ever? Did anyone ask me if I wanted to go to a stupid anniversary dinner on a Saturday night when everyone else in the known universe is out having a life?'

'It's very important to your mother. I think she's planning to reveal that we're the descendants of a long-lost branch of the Russian royal family. It is time, Tsar Alecovitch, we take back the throne.'

'It's not funny.' I throw myself face down in my pillow. 'It's like living in the middle ages. It's a wonder I have any friends at all. The guys probably think I'm a total freak.'

'That's good, isn't it?' She throws the pastel up in the air and catches it without even looking. Her hand—eye co-ordination is awesome. 'I bet all the kids who went to school with Jackson Pollock thought he was a nutbag. *Who does he think he bloody is? Constable?*'

'I guess.'

'It's a bitch, isn't it, being your age? I know. Hormones, girls, school, friends, pressure. It's a right pain in the arse.'

'As if you remember. When you were sixteen, pains in the arse were cured by leeches.'

'Ha. De. Ha.' She stands. 'Are you coming down or not?'

I'm coming. Grandpa is nearly here. I'm not cutting off my nose despite my face.

———✦———

I wish I was a writer. If I immortalised people in words instead of paint and pencil and digital images, I could sit quiet in the corner jotting away and no one would be the wiser. But drawing is a public business. *What are you doing, Alec? Oh, isn't that lovely? What's it supposed to be?* Ad. Frikkin. Nauseam.

So I don't sketch. Instead I concentrate on the scene in front of me so I can remember it later. Which wouldn't be necess-ary if I had a phone with a camera in it instead of an actual camera, an ancient relic which does nothing except take photos.

209

Speaking of relics: we are all sitting around the dining table. Grandpa is at one end, Uncle Frank is at the other. They look the same but different, the way Charlotte and Stanzi do. On the other side of the table, Libby is sitting between Charlotte and Stanzi. Grandma is sitting next to me.

'This is lovely, Charlotte,' says Grandma, around a mouthful of Charlotte's casserole, which looks like newspaper soaked in milk. She is wearing her pale blue dress, the one with the matching shoes and handbag that make her look like the Queen Mother. 'I'd almost think it was meat, if I didn't know better.'

'It's not meat?' says Uncle Frank. 'What is it then? I don't eat anything green, Charlotte. Vegetables are too hard on my colon.'

'Don't complain.' Grandpa, always dapper, is wearing a blue cravat that matches Grandma's dress. 'A tofu has given up its life for this meal.' He's smiling, but he doesn't eat much. Nothing like Charlotte's cooking to curve your appetite.

Now Uncle Frank is talking to Libby, which serves her right for being such a suck. He's telling her stories of the old days: about how they all used to live here. How it was our great-grandparent's house and then Uncle Frank's until I was born, and then he gave it to Charlotte and Stanzi and moved into the nursing home because by then the firm had let him go and he wanted to be around other people his own age. He loves it in the nursing home. Bowls, bingo. You name it. Libby's eyes are glazing over. Soon he'll get on to how tiny this house used to be before Grandma and Grandpa paid for the upstairs extension where me and Lib's rooms are.

How lame are Charlotte and Stanzi. There's no way I'm living in the family house when I'm grown up. I'm going to get the hell out of here and live in a loft in New York. Or India. I could backpack around India and speak Indian and do paintings of temples and the colours of saris and smiling babies.

Listening to Uncle Frank, Libby looks like she's about to lapse into a coma. Before they arrived she came up to me in the hall and she was all *this is so lame. Mission Impossible 3 is having advance screenings*, at which I almost laughed out loud. I was all *introducing the current Australian lame champion, MI3 being rank Hollywood commercialism featuring formulaic storytelling with pathetic CGI I want to see Scary Movie 4* and she nods, but it's out of the question because Charlotte will never let her. She's too much of a baby. She has nightmares.

The actual meal winds up early because if old people eat after 8pm and you get them wet they turn into gremlins. After we've cleared the plates, Grandpa stands up and clinks his fork against his glass and says, 'Ahem. I'd like to say a few words.'

Here we go. I love Grandpa and everything, but this will be an all-points Bore. Dom. Alert.

He starts to say how fifty years ago today was the best day in his long and happy life, because that was when he married *that beautiful girl sitting right there. Annabel Crouch.* Grandma blushes and raises her glass to him. Charlotte says *hear hear.* She has had two glasses of wine and is actually smiling.

'You've always been the lucky one, Kip,' says Uncle Frank. 'Midas touch.'

'And it means everything to me to have my brother here, and our two beautiful girls, and our two wonderful grandchildren.'

Yep. So far, so boring.

'You're wearing your mother's pendant Charlotte, I see.'

She smiles and opens her collar a little wider. Sure enough, there it is: the purple necklace she loves so much. 'Only for special occasions, Dad.'

'It has always disturbed me, though,' he says, 'that we had only one pendant and two daughters.'

'I took the money, Dad,' Stanzi says. 'You bought my first car. Remember?'

'Still. Your mother and I have decided that, although it's our anniversary, you two girls should get the presents.' Grandma rivals in her bag and pulls out an envelope and a small parcel and hands them to him. 'Here.'

The envelope is for Mum. There's cash in it, I can see from here. Enough to make Mum cry. She hugs everyone, even Uncle Frank. The parcel is for Stanzi: inside is an old-fashioned coin, dull silver, with a king's head on one side. It has a silver chain threaded through a hole in the middle. Stanzi looks like she's about to cry too.

'I loved looking at it, framed in my study,' says Grandpa. 'But I'm getting on. It's more important that it goes to you. It's a fine old coin, isn't it Stanzi? Let me have a last look.'

Stanzi passes him the coin on the chain and Grandpa goes through an extended rigamarole of looking for his glasses: checking his pockets and Grandma's bag. Eventually they decide he's left them in Stanzi's car.

'Alec,' he says. 'Can you run and get them? I think I left them under the front seat.'

'Of course he can,' Charlotte says. She hands me Stanzi's keys.

Outside, I take a minute to lean against the fence. I don't mind running errands for Grandpa. I mean, he's eighty. What am I supposed to do? Tell him to go get his own glasses?

It's dark now. Must be well past eight. It's weird to think of a different lot of Westaways living in this house. I try to imagine it as a 3D painting: Escher-style, one layer on top of another, different times, different people. I think about these other people with their old-fashioned clothes and hair, walking down hallways sleeping in beds. Ghosts walking among us.

Inside, around that table, everyone knows who they are. They know every drop of blood in their veins. Where they've come from, the features and gestures and traits that have been passed down. They take it for granted. Me and Libby, we're half Westaways. We don't know what belongs to the other side. All this looking backwards, it's a complete crock. Grandpa can track his blood. Uncle Frank's right: he's the lucky one.

I open the car door and kneel. The glasses are right where he said they'd be, but next to them is a parcel wrapped in bright blue paper, with a little card in an envelope. The envelope says: *Alec*. I open it. The card says, in a shaky old-person hand: *Tonight everyone gets a present! Though it's best to keep this just between us! All our love, Grandma and Grandpa*. I open the parcel and almost die of shock. Inside is a brand new Nintendo DS, still in the box.

I don't know how they knew the exact right thing to get, the perfect thing that would blow my mind, but they managed it. You, Grandma and Grandpa, officially, totally, rock. And *Just between us* is right. It won't last two minutes up in my bedroom with Libby and Mum around. I've got to hide it somewhere, and fast. They'll be expecting me back any second.

The front yard is so tiny, there's nowhere. I can't bury it, it'll get dirty. I open the gate and walk down the side of the house. There are some loose pavers stacked against the fence: I think about this for a bit, even move one, but it's all spiders and shit. I kneel down and run my hands along the bricks of the foundations. One of them looks a little loose, so I push a bit and—hey pesto! I lift the brick out and there's a decent space behind it. It looks about the right size, but the Nintendo won't go in. I drop my head for a good look and—hang on, there's already something in here. Carefully, I slide my hand inside. I lift it out.

<hr />

Back inside, I give Grandpa his glasses. Then I sit at the table, a little awkwardly. The Nintendo is in the letter box: I'll move it later, after everyone's gone. But I found this wicked thing and I have to show them.

'Get a load of this,' I say. 'I found it outside.'

In the middle of the table I place the tin. It's got a parrot eating a biscuit on the front and it's covered in tarnish and rust.

'Will you take a look at that,' says Grandma.

'God, it's filthy,' says Libby.

'Open it, Alec,' says Charlotte. 'You found it.'

So I do. I have to get my nails under the lid, it's a good tight fit, but inside, in a brown envelope, is a photograph. An old one, black and white, but the tones are vivid and crisp. There's a crush of people. A bunch of them are soldiers. In the middle is one particular soldier. He's leaning out of a train, out the window. You can see him really well: crew cut, uniform. He's stretching to kiss a girl. The girl is sitting on someone's shoulder and she's stretching up to him. You can't see her so good, just her old-fashioned wavy hair and her shape.

'Dad,' says Charlotte. 'Are you all right?'

———+———

First, he stared at the photo. He said nothing. There was just this look on his face, like his skin was melting. Then he stood, he made this weird noise. Then he fell.

For twenty minutes now, we've all been still. Grandpa is lying on the couch. Mum wanted to call an ambulance but he said no. *Don't fuss, Charlotte*, he said.

'If your father says he's fine, he's fine.' Grandma stirs his tea, clinks the spoon on the side.

'You collapsed. That doesn't sound fine to me,' says Charlotte.

'Stood up too quickly, that's all. Blood pressure,' says Uncle Frank.

Grandpa makes a face. 'Blood pressure? What rot.'

'Mum. What is it? What's going on?' says Libby.

'Don't, Kip. Not right to speak ill of the dead,' says Uncle Frank.

Grandpa sits up and pulls Libby half on to his lap. 'It's a love letter, sweetie. Except it's a photograph.' He says that in the olden days, things were different. *No one expected a grand passion, you see.* He squeezes Grandma's hand. *We aimed for smaller things: the health of our family, being warm, being safe.*

'I remember Ma saying that when Dad was alive we were so rich, it didn't matter how thickly she peeled the potatoes,' says Uncle Frank.

I hold the photo in my hands. It was the first one he ever took, Grandpa says. It was what made him decide to spend his life taking photos. From what he says, it seems like all kinds of stupid things had to be kept secret back then. When he says that his sister didn't die from the flu, Stanzi just nods. Charlotte gets on her high horse about *ridiculous sexist taboos* and *lies* and *nothing to be ashamed of*. Grandma smiles. *You can't imagine what it was like back then*, she says. *So much pain, all covered over.*

'And all this time you knew it was him,' says Uncle Frank. 'You never told a soul.'

'She asked me not to. I never knew she had this developed. She must've hid it herself.' Grandpa takes my hand: not like he's holding a little kid's, like he's shaking it, like I'm a man and he's pleased to meet me. 'This photo won't be out of my sight from now on. You've given me my sister back, Alec. She'd have liked you, and your art. Wherever she is, I'm sure she's looking out for you.'

216

Grandpa is feeling better so it's time for them to go home. Charlotte is bustling around getting Uncle Frank and Grandma into Stanzi's car, keeping Uncle Frank steady when he steps down from the footpath, folding Grandma's walker and fitting it in the boot, when she realises Grandpa's missing.

'Alec,' she says, and this means *Slave boy! Find him, toot sweet!*

Grandpa's not so good with stairs so he must be outside and that's where I find him, in the backyard, standing under the tree, feeling the bark like he's never seen a tree before. He looks about a thousand years old. He's skinnier than I remember and he bends over like his shoulders are too heavy. I want to tell him to push his chest out but I know he can't help it. I force my own shoulders back.

'The party bus is leaving. All aboard.'

'This is where I last saw her. Just here. Leaning against this tree, talking to my mother. She never met your mother or Stanzi. Never saw me marry Annabel. She was nineteen when she died. He must've been twenty-one.' He waves one arm at the trattoria across the lane.

'Grandpa. It's time to go home.'

'Right here. Under this tree.'

I take him by the arm and walk him back through the house. In the hallway he stops. He grabs my face with both hands, holds it tight and close with stronger fingers than I would have figured. He's strong for an oldie. I'm forced to look right into his eyes.

'Alec. You must know this. People disappear. They just go puff. Thin air. Every time you see someone, you never know if you're seeing them for the last time. Drink them in, Alec. Kiss them. It's very important. Never let anyone say goodbye, even for a little while, without kissing them. Press your lips against the people you love. Hands, they can touch anything. Open doors, hold cameras, hang clothes on the line. It's lips that matter.'

'Thin air. Last time. Kiss them. Lips. Got it.' I try to get him moving before Charlotte calls out again.

'You don't get it.' He releases the zombie death grip around my head, and he kisses me. 'Well, that's all right. I hope you never will.'

I think he's going to say something else, but he just keeps walking down the hall.

I watch him go. Standing beside the tree he looked frail. His skin is blotchy and dry like the bark, like someone has taken a fine brush and painted veins and bruises, white spots and dabs of red. Next to him my skin looks varnished, smooth.

When me and Libby were little, Grandpa was in charge of all the dad stuff. He took photos of us, hundreds of them. He still has them over at their apartment at the retirement village. He was the one who taught us to play poker and took us to the football.

I remember coming home from school once, crying. I would have been around six or seven. I was picked last for some team. That was me, the kid without the father, West the pest, Mr Unco. Grandma used to be here after school, to look after us while Mum and Stanzi were at work, and she called Grandpa and next thing I knew, he pulled up. He'd left some photoshoot, just left the model and the client standing there. *A family emergency*, he told them.

'Right,' he said, as he walked into my room. I was face down on my bed, head in the pillows, and the sound of his voice so startled me I rolled over and sat up. He took off his jacket and his tie and draped them on the door handle. 'Where's that boy who says he can't catch a ball?'

That autumn afternoon the air was cooling and he stood in the backyard with me for hours while the sun went down and threw a tennis ball at me. When it got dark and I'd mastered his gentle underarm lobs, he moved us to Rowena Parade and parked his car up on the footpath and put the headlights on. Even when Grandma said *that boy's had enough*, he kept at it. By the end, I was thirsty and tired and my shoulders were aching and he was throwing it hard and fast and high and I was catching it, every single time. He didn't let me quit. I was never picked last for sport again.

After Grandpa kisses us all and they leave, it's quiet at home, just the three of us. Stanzi will drop them off at their retirement home, then go out with her friends. She won't be home for hours, maybe not until morning. Charlotte is tired from the cooking and she decides to clean up tomorrow. We're just going to bed, when we turn our heads and see it together. The photo of Connie at the train station is on the couch. I don't know how we didn't notice her before.

'Oh, no. When Dad realises it's missing, he'll be frantic.' Charlotte looks straight at me.

'I'll take it back to him tomorrow.'

'He was so happy to have that photo. He's so frail.'

'First thing in the morning. As soon as I get up. Off I'll go.'

'He said he wouldn't let it out of his sight. He said his sister's been returned to him.'

'Just ring Stanzi's mobile. She can't have gotten far. Ask her to come back and pick it up.'

'I will not. If she wants to get a brain tumour that's her business but I will not be contributing to it.'

'OK, OK. I'll go. I'll ride my bike.' Not like there's anything fun to do around here anyway.

'You will not. It's too dark.'

This is an example of the futility of my life. *Go*, she says. *All right*, I say. *No*, she says. It's insane.

'It's all the way to Kew. It's two trams. I'm tired. I won't be back before eleven.'

'Alec. He's old. What if he dies tonight? What if this was the last time you ever saw him and you had a chance to do something kind for someone who's done so much for you, and you didn't take it? How would you live with yourself?'

Grant me strength. 'He's not going to die tonight. How do you function in the world, thinking like that?'

'Alec.' She makes her eyes go big and round like some manga puppy, which is her standard manipulation technique. 'Please. You won't have to do any dishes tomorrow. No drying, no wiping. Libby will even take the bins out.'

'What? Libby will what?' Libby says, in her most whiney

220

voice. 'Muuuum. That is totally unfair. I can go to Grandpa's. I don't mind.'

That's it then. 'All right, all right,' I say. 'I'll go.'

It must be around nine when I walk down Lennox Street to Bridge Road. If I was on my bike, I'd go via Victoria: that part of Richmond is way cooler, like being in Saigon. Trust my olds to live on the hill in the boring Anglo part. Connie is back in her envelope, back in the biscuit tin, safe in my backpack. Bridge Road is still crowded: the pubs and clubs and restaurants are full, people are milling about, but there's no one else waiting for the tram. I'm standing at the stop alone when I hear a horn.

In front of the tram stop, the hottest car I have ever seen in my whole entire life pulls up. It's mad crimson, so shiny it looks wet, low to the ground. A hotted-up Ford, chrome mags, Eminem blaring, the whole chassis trembling from the woofers. The front window goes down. Ohmigod. It's Tim.

'Lecster. Mate. Get the fuck in the car.'

All the windows go down now. It's Tim's brother Andy driving, big grin on his face. Andy's living proof of exactly how dumb my mother is. She is always on at me about doing good at school, about having something to fall back on if art doesn't work out. And here is Andy, an apprentice plumber, proud owner of a fully sick car and let me assure you he is no rocket surgeon. I could leave school right now and get any job and do just fine. In the back seat are Cooper and Wade and

Henry. I can see their grinning faces inside. I say hi.

'Nice car. New?'

'I just picked it up,' says Andy. 'Just this second.' He laughs like a loon, snorting through his nose.

'Westie,' Cooper yells. 'Road trip. We is goin' to Rye.'

'We was just coming to your place,' says Tim, 'when we saw you waiting here for us. Forward thinking, brother.'

'We weren't going to park out the front,' says Cooper, tapping his temple. 'We learned our lesson.'

'We had it all planned. Park around the corner, send Tim in to ask if you could sleep over,' says Wade. 'No need to alarm the hippy Oberführer.'

'We got beer.' Henry lifts up what looks like the best part of an entire slab.

'Plenty of room,' yells Andy, from the driver's seat. 'Get in and have a brew.'

This, ladies and gentlemen, is living. Driving in a hot red car down to the beach with your mates, watching the sun come up over the water, drinking beer, talking shit. God, maybe we'll meet some girls down there. Not city girls, beach girls. Easter holidays are only just over. Not too cold for bikinis, not quite. I've wasted my whole entire existence up to now. I've done absolutely nothing with it. I've just been counting down the months of my life. Sixteen years, totally useless. I live with three women. A big night at my place is when the ABC runs a Jane Austen marathon. God I hate that Bennet chick. Marry him already, spare us all the drama!

Tonight, in contrast, could well be the greatest night of my life. I can almost feel the sand, smell the sea. This would be

222

a bond we share forever: me and Tim and Andy and Cooper and Wade and Henry. I'd have made it. I'd be one of the guys.

Cooper opens the back seat. On the floor of the car is something the colour of cardboard; it stands out against the white carpet. And then I smell it. Oh. My. God. Pizza. There is pizza in that car. Actual, non-homemade, non-wholemeal pizzas that have never seen a vegetable in their entire cheesy lives. With artificial flavourings and actual meat, from an animal.

'Westaway,' Cooper says. 'Get in. For once in your life, do not be a pussy.'

I have my hand on the door when I feel the strap of my backpack. I'd forgotten about Connie.

Could I ask the guys to swing past the retirement home first? Ah, no. That would be utterly lame. I can fully imagine the copious amount of shit they'd give me. *Westie needs to go see his gramps. What a good boy you are, Westie.* I've heard it all before. At primary school, half the class would chant *Westie's testes aren't the bestie*. Everyone said my balls were permanently shrunken from the chick pheromones in the air at my place. Once, in year eight, I found out that everyone thought I was lying about Charlotte and Stanzi being sisters. They all thought they were gay, that I had two mums, and they started saying I was gay too. Charlotte had to go see the principal. And if I told the guys about the photo of my great aunt? Even if they didn't think I was a softcock, which they would, they'd say *Bros before hos*. Andy revs the engine.

'Brother that light's not gonna get any greener,' says Tim. 'Get in.'

223

'Hey, s'cool. Westie's not interested in beer and cars,' says Andy. 'We all know he likes drawing pretty pictures. He's more a stay-home-and-watch-Oprah-with-the-girls kinda guy.'

'Not that there's anything wrong with that.' Cooper sniggers.

I want to get in the car. I do. But *What if he dies tonight? What if this was the last time you ever saw him?* I will my legs to move but instead I think about Grandpa, how frail he looked and the colours in his skin. About the things he was saying to me, about that tennis ball he threw at me for hours when I was a little kid. I think about what he said to me in the hall. *Every time you see someone, you never know if you're seeing them for the last time.*

That's it. I am without a doubt the biggest moron in the history of moronness. My entire life is completely fucked.

'Nah,' I say. 'I got shit to do.'

Like quitting school and giving away all my possessions and joining an Antarctic expedition where I end up freezing my dick off and eating my own dog.

'Westicle,' says Tim. 'Surely you jesticle, testicle.'

'Busy,' I say.

'One-time offer, Westie,' says Cooper. 'Get in the car now or forever be known as a piker.'

Yep. Fucked. For. Ever. Thanks, Charlotte. Thanks Grandpa. 'Thanks anyway.'

'You are such a fucking loser,' says Cooper. They all lean out the windows near me, doing the shape of Ls on their foreheads.

'Can't argue with that,' I say. 'Have a nice time.'

I wave as they hoon off. An empty beer can zips out of a back window, hits me square on the knee and clatters against the tram stop. The dregs dribble out on the cement. I watch the car hum and throb and all the way to the lights, the heads of people on the street spin to look as it passes. It is the most alive thing in the whole street, the whole suburb. For a long way before they turn, I see the crimson paintwork reflected in puddles on the road and it's like, for a second, there's a real car and a ghost one, both of them speeding down Bridge Road, leaving me and the photo far behind.

———+———

At the maximum security facility for the ancient and infirm, I have to punch a number in to the keypad near the door like it was an ATM. Please enter your six-digit PIN and select the gerie you'd like to withdraw. Your remaining gerie balance will appear on the screen. What fucked security, I think, because the number is printed out on a laminated sheet stuck right to the front door. Anyone who could read the number could get in. And then I realise: it's meant to stop the demented old buggers getting out, because presumably they can't read and/or punch numbers.

That. Is. So. Shit. I feel so sad for Grandpa and Grandma and even Uncle Frank. Mum looked for months to find a place they could stay together, and this was the best she could find, but they're not demented. It's close to us and it's the best place for them, Mum said. We can't separate them now.

At the front desk they ring up to Grandpa's room then send me up. He's standing in the doorway in his pyjamas, waiting.

'What is it? What's happened?'

'Nothing. I thought I'd hang with you guys for a while. I hear there are lots of single chicks.'

'You wouldn't last five seconds.' Grandma appears in the doorway behind him, hair in rollers with a net over the top. I thought no one did that in real life, that rollers were only in old movies. How does she sleep in them? It'd be like having acupuncture all over your scalp. 'They're barracudas,' she says. 'They'd eat you alive.'

Grandpa says, 'They can smell tender young flesh. You should run while you still can.'

I lift the backpack off my shoulders and take out the tin. 'Plus I thought I'd drop this off.' I open it, take it out of the envelope, hold the photo carefully with both hands.

'Oh dear.' Grandpa puts both hands to his face and sways a bit. For a moment I think he's going to faint. 'My sister.'

'Kip. You can't have forgotten Connie.'

'I must have. I didn't even realise she was missing.'

Wait, *what*? What did he say? He didn't even know she was missing? I turn down a road trip with the guys and ruin my entire life for all eternity, I haul myself all the way over here, two tram rides, thinking he'd be frantic, and he didn't even know she was missing? I could be eating pizza and drinking beer by now. Fuck, fuck, *fuck*. I smack my head against the door post.

'You're a good boy to drop her back.' Grandma kisses me on the cheek, then takes her from me and cradles her in her arms. 'What's wrong? Do you have a headache? Do you want an aspirin? Come in. Have some tea. We have Monte Carlos. It'll just be between us. We won't breathe a word.'

'Thanks anyway. Colonel Klink is waiting.'

'One cup,' says Grandpa. 'One biscuit. Two minutes. *We see nussink. We hear nussink.*'

What the hell. I could go home and watch a repeat of *Veronica Mars* on the couch with Libby, or I could go in. The whole apartment smells of old person but I don't mind that. I not only have one cup of tea, I have two goddammit. And four proper biscuits from a real plastic packet. Before long, Grandma goes to bed and I sit up with Grandpa, just talking. He tells me about the old days, about some horse he used to have, about the trouble Uncle Frank got up to when he was my age, but he also asks lots of questions about school and art. He's ace, actually. He understands what it's like for a brother to be outnumbered by women. The whole time he's talking, he has the photo of Connie in his hands. He never once puts her down.

I imagine what it would be like never to see Libby again, never have a chance to say goodbye to her. As much as she utterly shits me, that would suck. While Libby is alive I know I'll never really be alone. All the things I remember, every-thing about my life, our family, my childhood: it's all real because Libby knows it too.

The stuff he's talking about, though, the people-disap-pearing-never-to-be-seen-again stuff? That only happened back in the olden days. War and shit.

I can justify it all I like, but on the way home I suddenly

realise: I just spent Saturday night sitting in a retirement home with an old man in his eighties instead of being on the beach at Rye with my friends. The guys are right. I am a fucking loser.

———✦———

'Alec!' Mum yells, as soon as I turn my key in the lock. 'Where in God's name have you been? You should have been home hours ago.'

I thought she'd be way asleep by now, but she's standing in the hallway in her daggiest pyjamas staring, because apparently I have to account for every second of my time. Why doesn't she just get me an electronic ankle bracelet? She could significantly reduce her contribution to global warming by not asking where I've been every two freakin seconds.

I start to say *You know where I've been, to Grandpa's. You sent me.* My friends—in fact my ex-friends, past tense—my friends are down at Rye, sitting on the beach, eating pizza and drinking beer and I'm right here, but before I know it she's holding me. She's stretching up and she has her arms around my neck and she's gripping me for dear life, like she's drowning. I start to complain. I try to pull away. I'm sixteen years old, I'm not a baby. Then all at once it hits me: *my mother is smaller than me.*

She's tiny. I don't know the last time she held me like this, but I could reach down and wrap my arms around her and pick her up. So I do, for a moment, just to see if I can. I lift her right off the floor and she's dangling in the air. I'm hit

228

with this dizzy feeling that throws sparkles in front of my eyes. Fuck. I'm bigger than her. It's kind of terrifying. I'll be bigger than her for ever now. She'll get smaller and smaller like Grandpa until she dies and then she'll be gone and I won't have her anymore.

'Alec, sweetheart.'

'Shh, Mum. It's all right. I'm here.'

She's hardly letting me breathe. She's holding me so tight, pulling my face down to her neck so that I only have vision from one corner of my eye.

'There was a horrible car accident on the late news,' she's saying. 'Young boys, on the Monash freeway. Two dead, three critical. I just felt so sad for their families. They're only your age. I thought about what would happen if I ever lost you. And then I couldn't stop crying.'

I hug her again and she makes a big sigh. And it's only then, from that corner of my eye, that I see the crimson.

On that old-fashioned television, in that shabby house where I've lived all my life, being held by my tiny mother, I see that exact shade of crimson on the flickering screen.

I raise my head and she lets me go. I walk over to the TV.

'Alec. What is it?'

I drop to my knees and reach forward and touch the screen with my fingertips, like I could reach through the glass. Crimson is the colour of the wreck, the colour of what remains of the car's panels where they've wrapped around the light pole. Part of it is covered by a tarp but there it is: that colour, the mags, the twisted shape of it. And I see the police gathered around the crumpled metal, the lights flashing, the

229

fire truck a deeper red in the background. A policeman is being interviewed now, about the tragedy, about drinking, speeding, P-plate drivers, suspected stolen cars. About the senseless loss of young lives, about the devastation it will bring to the families who will never hold their sons again. My mother is speaking now and so is Libby, but I can't make out what they're saying. My fingertips touch the dark grey of the bitumen and the white blankets that are covering the mounds on the ground, the mounds that once were people.

Then the picture disappears and we're back to the studio. The newsreader looks sad, which is her job. Soon there will be a happier story and she'll perk up again. For her, this is just another accident among the hundreds she'll report every year. It means nothing that these people have vanished into thin air and will never be seen again. The names of the victims, the newsreader says in her professional way, have not yet been released.

CHAPTER NINE

Connie

THE RAIN IS coming. It's a mild night for winter but I can feel it even through the cold. The air is heavy, the way it laps against my skin. I raise my arms and it feels like I'm swimming in deep, still water instead of lying on my bed. Any minute now the weight will be too much for the air to hold and it will fall out in fat drops on the roof. Already there's a grassy, dewy smell. A distant memory of the ocean, a lingering of salt. Tonight this house doesn't even feel like Richmond. I could shut my eyes and be in St Kilda, or somewhere even further. Perhaps I did drift off for a little bit. It takes me a moment to remember where I am.

Ma does not notice the feeling of the air. I peek around the wardrobe and there she is in her bed, lying in the same position as she fell asleep in hours ago, a mound under her blankets, her hands in prayer under her left cheek. She sleeps like a child. It's a blessing, that type of surrender. One I have not been granted. All night my mind races, my feet wriggle. Even when I stretch out I can't seem to lie still.

I reach under the bed for my slippers. It's useless lying here, twitching and kicking. In the hall, I pause outside the boys' room. Francis is snoring and I can't see Kip's face: he's wedged a pillow over his head as usual. I open the front door to smell the air. It's freezing. There is a figure across the road under the street light. A tall man, leaning, thinking. It's Jack Husting.

I shut the door and turn back down the hall. In our room, I stand beside my bed, brush the back of my hand against the sheets. They're cold. It'll be light in a few hours and I have a big day at work tomorrow. Today. I should really get some sleep. I almost fold the sheets down and climb back snug inside. Instead I lift my nightgown over my head and slip on the dress hanging on the back of the door.

This time when I open the front door I feel his eyes on me. He watches as I walk closer, his head nods a fraction with each step I take. I look each way before I cross the street: a silly gesture. At this hour there's no one about but him and me.

And now here we are, together in the dark, me in my coat and slippers, him in trousers and a white shirt with the sleeves rolled up to just below his elbows. How he's not shivering I

232

don't know. He's a good six inches taller with the five o'clock shadow of a grown man before shaving. We are quiet for a long time.

'Are you really here?' Jack says. 'Or are you sleepwalking?'

'I'm not sure. I feel like part of me is asleep and part is awake. Does it matter?'

'Too right it does.' His voice is a raspy whisper, low and soft. He digs both hands in his pockets and looks up at the stars. 'If you're awake I'll take a bit of care about what I say. Don't want you to think I'm a dill tomorrow.'

'And if I'm asleep?'

'Then odds are you'll forget all about this by the morning. And I am free to make a fool of myself.'

I smile. Jack Husting is not the kind of man who would ever make a fool of himself. 'Then I'm asleep. Besides, it doesn't matter what I think. Your leave's over. You're off tomorrow.'

'That's true.' He rubs one hand down his arm like he can feel it too, the pressure in the air. 'Tomorrow I'm off.'

In our houses, just a few dozen yards away, our families are sound asleep. We're alone out here in the dark. Just for now, it's a separate world we're standing in and we're the only two alive in it. The street lamp throws a circle of light. Perhaps that's as far as our world extends.

'How did your mum take it, you signing up?'

'It's hard for her. She's not coming to the station to see me off. Dad neither. Took them by surprise, I suppose.'

'That's the difference between men and women.' I watch his face, tanned and angular under the light. There's a tension in the way he holds his arms. He's pretending to be relaxed. 'We women do what's expected. You can do almost anything you care to think of.'

He shakes his head. 'I reckon that depends on the woman, and the man.'

I feel a drop on my cheek. The air can't hold the water anymore.

'Oh no.' I hold one hand out flat, fingers pressed together, to give the sky a chance to change its mind. 'I'm not ready to go in yet.'

Ready or not, before I finish speaking, thousands of drops are smacking against us, against the street, the houses and the fences. Sheets of water, all let loose. Loud too. My coat is wet through already, my cotton dress is sticking to my shoulders and thighs.

'Come on.' Jack has to shout and before I know it he is holding my hand in his bigger one and we are running, pelting across the street and around the corner and down the side of the shop, threading our way down the narrow concrete path, past the azaleas and the camellias that line the path. Their leaves are glossy and dark. Our palms are slippery from the rain. In the backyard, he lets go of me and I wrap my arms around my middle and shiver while he slides open the door to the stable. Inside, it's dry and warmer than I'd expected, though the sound is even louder on the iron roof. The torrent is like a glass wall in the open door.

'You need a blanket.' He rifles through a pile at the back on top of the hay.

'I'd rather be wet than smell of horse.'

Charlie gives a mild snort and looks at me with liquid eyes. 'You've offended him.' Jack scratches his nose. 'She didn't mean it. You smell delightful.'

'If you think that, you spent too long on that station.'

'I did spend too long. I should have come home years ago. If I'd known about the neighbours, I would have.'

'Is that so?' I say, and it's all I can do to stop my hands from shaking. 'What is it about the neighbours that would have brought you home? They're a shady lot, I suppose? Perhaps you didn't think your parents were safe?'

'I'm the one who's not safe, Connie,' he says. He runs his hand along the side of Charlie's face and Charlie nuzzles him back.

I take off my coat and squeeze the water out, then I fold my arms and look out the window at the rain. 'Yet tomorrow you're off. Enlisted of your own free will, did you?'

'It seemed a good idea.'

'I'm sure it was. I'm sure you'll have all kinds of adventures. See the world, fight for King and country, all that. You won't have time to spare a thought for us at home.'

'You'll be busy soon, as well.' He turns away from Charlie and faces me, arms folded just like mine. 'Your ma is telling anyone who'll listen that you'll be engaged to that newspaper man any day now. What's his name again? Bored?'

'It's Ward. And she's getting a bit ahead of herself, if she's said that.'

'Ah,' he says, like I've just explained the workings of the internal combustion engine. 'Like that, is it?'

The rain seems not so heavy now, a dull background hum.

'It's eased up. I'll make a run for it.'

'Don't.'

'You can't give me orders. I'm not one of your soldier boys.'

'You're right.' He walks over and stands right in front of me, inches away. 'Don't, please.'

It's time to go back to my own bed, to the room I share with Ma. It really is. Time to go.

'You're still wet.' With one hand he lifts the sleeve of my dress up to the top of my shoulder, then he runs the flat of his fingers down my arm, a gentle even pressure. He stops at the elbow and flicks off the water. 'You'll catch your death.'

'Jack.'

This time he reaches both hands out and holds my dress at the waist, a hand at either side. He scrunches it in his brown fists so that it's tight around me, he squeezes the fabric. Two tiny trickles of water fall to the ground.

'It's you I think about,' he says. 'Every night when I can't sleep, when I walk the streets. Tonight it's like I've conjured you up.'

I look in his eyes and it's a mistake. They're soft, the colour of dark honey. There are all kinds of thoughts buzzing, things I should say, should do, but I can't move. I just look, and then it feels like falling.

He pulls the dress now, little movements but strong. I can see his forearms tense, the muscle firm under the sodden white of his shirt, and I move towards him. Tiny steps, in my slippers. My arms are limp until I'm right up against him, pressing against him down to my toes. Then my traitor arms lift and rest against his chest.

'Just let me kiss you, Connie. I'd die a happy man.'

I barely move my head. He leans down closer, closer. He brushes the side of his face against mine—it's rough, it stings and prickles. I feel his open mouth on one side of mine, feel his wetness and his breath, and I try to be still but it's more than I can bear. Before I know it I'm on my tiptoes, arms around his neck. I'm kissing him back.

This kissing. The smell of him, the taste. I'm in Jack Husting's arms and he's holding me and there's a fierceness I've never felt before. I can't get enough air but it's not air I'm wanting. He's twisting me to my side, cradling me. He kisses the side of my mouth, the line of my chin, the space behind my ear and my mouth, over and over. I raise my head when I feel about to topple over and he puts a hand behind to steady himself. We start to sink and he sits on the floor, back against the wall, and I'm across his lap.

'Connie,' he says, into my neck. 'I've got to send you back to your own bed.'

'Yes.' He raises his head and I find his throat with my teeth. 'That'd be for the best.'

'It just won't do.' He brushes the side of my breast with his hand and when I say nothing, only draw air into my lungs in a whoosh, he cups one breast and it's heavy and full in his hand, the perfect shape to fit there. 'It's not right, Connie. We should wait.'

'Yes,' I say. 'Wait.' My teeth close over his skin.

With his right hand, he undoes the buttons at the top of my dress. One. Two. Three. He slides his hand inside and he bows his head as he does it, like a man praying. His thumb darts across my nipple, flicking the nub of it. Jesus Mary and Joseph. So this is what it is. What men and women get up to in their beds at night. He moves us a little so I'm resting against the hay.

'This far and no further,' he says. His voice is all crackles and sighs.

But it will not be *this far and no further*. I will not let it be. Inside of me there is a heat. I want his hands on the inside of my thigh, I want to see them there, I want to feel it. I want, I want. I can hardly breathe for the wanting. It seems that all my life I've had nothing I've desired and I've given up having desires at all. Now I know what it feels like to want and I will give anything to have it. I can hardly form the thoughts but there's a wetness at my core and a hardness at his and I feel a rush of something I've never known: a power. I am queen of a distant land and everything is at my command. I slip my tongue in the corner of his mouth and he groans like pain. I push my whole body against him and part of me watches him search for control but I know he will not find it, not here, not now. I tug his shirt from his trousers and he closes his eyes and tilts his head back. The world is mine.

'Jack,' I say.

He is helpless before me. I touch his belt and my nerve falters but he follows my thoughts and does it himself: he unbuckles, readies himself, slides my dress up to my waist and I feel the air on myself down there. He is staring at me yet it's his body that's beautiful, the most beautiful thing I've ever seen. As he closes in on me I feel a sudden panic, a fear of pain, and yes there's pain but it's sweet and sharp and it fades into more wanting and more and he's still as stone for a while. And soon, again, the stillness is unbearable and it's my wanting that drives us. I see now the closeness between these words: 'wanting' and 'wanton'. I move my hips under him, circle and thrust. I cannot help it. There is simply nothing else that can be done.

'Connie,' Jack says. 'Be still for God's sake,' but I will not. I raise my hips to meet him and together we plunge and grind and his face is a contortion of losing himself in me and for a few blessed minutes we are utterly together, meeting one another with our limbs and our mouths and our skin and our sweat and our breath. The feeling is impossible, astounding. No other living soul has ever felt this way.

'I'm not asking you to wait,' he says. 'Do you hear me? I'm not asking you.'

I am buttoning my dress, daring myself to stand. It seems that all the life has drained from my legs: they can barely take my weight. It's a wonder that married women can stand at all, much less walk. He has brought some water in an old mug from out in the yard and I've made a shoddy try at cleaning myself and I've dried off with a towel.

'I can hear you.' My thighs are sticky. The sun will be up any moment. I need to get home and run a bath.

'You have a life all planned out,' he says.

'All planned out by my mother.'

'I'm going to war.'

'I understand.'

'I've got nothing to offer you,' he says.

'I know,' I say. 'Just come back.'

His shirt has hay sticking stuck to one side and his trousers look like they've never seen an iron. He runs one hand through his hair and transfers more hay to it. 'It'd be some pretty poor kind of love if I didn't want what was best for you,' he says.

I stop fidgeting with my dress and turn to look at him. 'Is that how it is.'

'It doesn't matter how it is. I'm going off, Christ, in just a few hours. You're here and you've got to do what's best for everyone.'

I stand in front of him and run my finger along the line of his jaw and down the cliff of his chin and along the beauty of his throat. I can feel him swallow under the pad of my finger and he squeezes his eyes tight for a moment.

'Although,' he says, 'the whole show will probably be over in a few months and then I'll be back.'

'Could be.'

He clears his throat. 'And if you were free when I got back, if you were free by some chance, I'd spend all my years becoming the kind of man you'd deserve.'

'Would you now.'

'Hypothetically.'

'Hypothetically. Your mother would have a pink fit.'

'More like deep magenta.' He laughs. 'She's had her time. Now belongs to you and me.' He kisses me again, deep and long. 'And Connie,' he says. 'I do have one thing to ask you.'

On the platform, I walk among the crowd of strangers and somehow nobody knows. No one stops and stares, no one points. It isn't possible I look the same as I did yesterday, I just can't. But Kip is standing beside me and even he can't tell. He speaks to me like he would any other day. Even when I got out of the bath this morning, even though it's not my usual bath day, Ma straightaway asked me if we had any eggs and where did I put the starch. Not one scrap of me is the same yet they notice nothing different at all.

'Look at all these people,' says Kip. 'And so many soldiers! Be a wonder if they all fit on the train.'

As well as becoming a woman, I am now suddenly someone who can design things for her own ends. It was a simple matter to be here at the station: Mr Ward is keen on my ideas and agreed that the embarkation of part of the second AIF for North Africa would make a fine picture for the *Argus*. There's no photographer here yet. One is on his way after another job at a fire on the other side of town. I have a spare camera with me in case he's run out of film, and I have the camera ready: out of its case, and I've set up the aperture and shutter speed. The lens I've chosen is wide enough to get most of the train. Kip is here because he has the day off from the Hustings, who have have shut the shop to weep in peace over Jack's departure, and because I asked him to come. Kip being here will ensure I behave. In a group of strangers, I don't trust myself not to cry.

Kip's right about the crowd; it's huge and growing. There are all sorts of people here: an older woman in a wide-brimmed hat holding a baby in a bonnet; men in their sharpest suits; a group of young women also dressed up to the nines, hankies to their eyes already; police and station guards patrolling. A whistle blows. The train is leaving. All the soldiers give one last look around and the stragglers climb on board. I'd thought we'd have more time than this. We've only just made it.

'Would you look at that.' Kip grabs my arm and points his own. 'There's Jack Husting.'

He's leaning out of the train window in uniform: khaki with big square pockets, a strap across his chest holding his swag in place. He's looking everywhere. He is searching for someone.

'So it is,' I say.

'Jack, Jack!' Kip yells.

His head spins and he sees us. I curse bringing Kip because now I don't care a fig what anyone thinks. I want to run to Jack, hold him tight, beg him not to go.

'Connie!' Jack waves one arm above his head, out the window.

'The train's leaving,' says Kip. 'And the photographer's still not here.'

In front of the train, the crowd is milling and jostling. If I just fit through that gaggle of people, I can reach him.

'Here,' I say to Kip, and I take the strap of the camera and hang it around his neck. He sags a little then straightens at once: he wasn't expecting the weight of it. 'Just hold the camera, all right? Stay out of the crush and don't let anything happen to it. And don't touch anything. Especially not here.' I point to the shutter release button, so he knows, so there's no confusion.

'As if I would,' he says.

Any moment now Jack'll be gone. I run to the crowd, I thread my way through, using my elbows, pushing like a fishwife. He is still there, leaning from the window. I can see his mouth form words he doesn't say, I can see him swallow. I reach up and he takes my hand. We look and look, but looking and hands aren't enough. I wedge one foot against the rail of the train but it's too thin. I can't gain enough footing to hold my weight and any moment now the train'll start to move and if I don't watch it I'll fall between the carriage and the platform. All at once I notice a soldier beside me, an older man in the same uniform. He's as tall as Jack, or taller. He's seeing someone off.

'He's a lucky soldier.' The man gestures to Jack, who is by now leaning so far out of the window I fear he'll fall on his head on the platform. 'Need a hand, miss?'

And I can hardly believe it, but the man squats nearly to the ground and wraps an arm around my waist and as he stands—Lord!—I'm hoisted in the air like a small child, sitting on the shoulder of some stranger. I must be more than eight foot off the ground. I grasp a handle on the train door to steady myself but the man is strong all right. He has a big grin on his face and he gives my rump a squeeze.

'Go on then,' he says.

I do go on. Jack doesn't say anything, and neither do I.

243

Everything that can be said's already said. I reach up, and Jack reaches down, and I kiss him. I'm the one kissing him. I've come this far, I've fought through the crowd. I feel his lips and the touch of it lasts and lasts and just when I think I'll drop off my perch with dizziness, I hear the whistle and the stranger kneels and I'm standing and the train is pulling out. There's nothing but a blur except for Jack's eyes, Jack's face. I don't stop looking until the train is gone.

I blink. The stranger is gone, the people are gone, the train is long gone. I'm hit with a sudden fear: what if I forget his exact expression? The look in his eyes, the line of his jaw? It might be months before I see him again. What happens if I forget that a kiss can last forever? Somehow I keep my head upright, then I feel a tug on my sleeve. Kip is standing beside me.

'I did exactly what you told me,' he says, camera still around his neck. 'I didn't touch a thing.'

———————✦———————

The Lord only knows what will happen. Every night I lie here, in my own bed, in the room I share with my mother. Kip and Francis are asleep next door; if I listen close I'll hear Francis's snoring. I know every squeak of every bedspring, I know the wardrobe is heavy timber with a bevelled mirror in the centre and you need to lift the door a little when you open it because it's sunk on its hinges.

The secret to happiness is to be grateful. I think about Ma, widowed with three children, and Nan who was a slave all her life, first in domestic service, then to Pop, then back to the ironing factory when she was widowed. I have a wonderful job. I have my mother and Francis, and I have Kip, my darling Kip.

And here is the most wonderful thing of all. I have had one night with the man of my heart and, just this once, I have had something that I wanted. Whatever happens, I will keep this night stored away like the linen in my glory box, his breath on my skin, the small hollow at the base of his throat soft on my lips. I will have that night forever. I can hardly believe my good fortune. Everything will be all right.

Acknowledgments

Early readers have the worst job in publishing, trudging their way through lumpen, leaden first drafts. My sincere thanks to mine. I've also been blessed with the generous research helpers Margaret Klaassen, Lee Falvey, Judy Stanley-Turner, Nada Lane and Katherine Sheedy. Clare Renner kindly donated the name Kip, which set the ball rolling. Kevin Culliver took the time and trouble to gently correct my many errors about the early years of St Kevin's College.

I've never met Kate Darian-Smith or Janet McCalman but I owe them both a drink or three; their respective books *On the Home Front* and *Struggletown* were heaven-sent and I recommend them for more information on Melbourne during the Second World War and on Richmond—and as great reads besides. All errors are, of course, my own.

At Text Publishing, the inimitable Mandy Brett was her usual patient, exacting self and was a joy to work with. The support of Jane Novak, Anne Beilby and Kirsty Wilson kept me going on dark days, so thanks.

I'm not one of those writers who have ideas banked up like circling planes awaiting their turn to land. My creative brain is more like a desert across which the odd ball of tumbleweed occasionally rolls. Michael Heyward understands this, and I just want to say thanks.